THE WILD MAN OF CAPE COD

THE WILD MAN OF CAPE COD

FRED MacISAAC

ILLUSTRATED BY
SAMUEL CAHAN

COVER BY
C.C. BEALL

POPULAR PUBLICATIONS · 2023

TABLE OF CONTENTS

THE WILD MAN OF CAPE COD

*What would you do if your fortune were
swept away and your fiancée jilted you?
Steve Cobb's idea was all right until—*

1

CAPE COD BEACHCOMBER

IT WAS ONE of those soft sweet summer days on Cape Cod when the South wind was blowing gently but steadily and causing good sized waves to roll upon the golden sands of Cobbport. Out in the bay a few fishing boats were bobbing lazily and away to the east a squadron of small yachts were making a race of it.

Stephen Cobb lay stretched out on the sand, a battered straw hat tipped over his face. He was naked save for scanty swimming trunks. A giant in bronze with honey colored hair. He measured six feet four did Steve Cobb and weighed two hundred and twenty and didn't have an ounce of fat on him. He lay flat neither asleep nor awake. The past was dead, the future didn't interest him much, and he hadn't done any thinking for ever so long. He became aware that somebody was prodding him in the side with the toe of a shoe and he grunted and opened his gray eyes.

"Come on. Wake up," somebody said sharply.

He tossed away the old straw hat and sat up. There was a young woman standing over him and his first impression of her was pleasant. This was a shapely young woman with a lot of yellow hair and fine features and blue eyes. Her mouth, however, was not smiling and her eyes were hostile.

"Well?" inquired Steve blandly.

"This is a private beach," she said significantly.

"Ask me if I care and listen intently for my response," he said with a broad grin.

"You have no business here. You are trespassing!" she exclaimed.

The man fell backward.

Her attitude was not so hostile now because he had very white teeth and a decent nose and nice eyes, while his almost naked figure was positively beautiful.

"Who the heck are you?" he asked quizzically.

"I own this beach—at least my father does. We propose to fence it in and keep loafers out."

"This beach belongs to the Cobb estate. Nobody has lived in the house for years. I kind of like this beach, lady."

"What are you? A clam digger?" she demanded.

"Part time. Part time fisherman."

*Steve's fist
had crashed his
left temple.*

She eyed him sharply. "You talk like an educated young man."

He nodded. "Compulsory education in Massachusetts. Too bad."

"Why that's what my father says. It's a mistake to educate the lower classes. It makes them discontented."

"Not me. I'm very contented."

"What's your name?"

"Cobb."

She half smiled. "Practically anonymous. Nearly all the natives are named Cobb."

"The original Cobb was some boy," remarked the beach-comber.

She frowned. "That will do. Kindly leave."

"Nope. I like it." He had been sitting up but now he lay down again and placed his hands behind his head and grinned at her insolently. "Take a tip, will you?"

"I'm beginning to get angry," she said menacingly.

"The tip is that a girl like you should wear fluffy summer dresses or a one-piece bathing suit. Those white pants you have on disfigure you."

The young lady stamped her foot. "This is too much!" she exclaimed. "Leave here at once or I'll get servants to drive you away."

"Here's an idea," he remarked. "Sit down beside me and I'll tell you the story of my life."

She turned and ran inshore.

"Snippy little snob," he observed aloud. "Oughtn't to wear pants. No girl ought to wear pants."

He closed his eyes and relaxed so completely that he dozed.

"There he is," a woman's voice cried shrilly. "Eject him, please."

Steve Cobb sat up. The girl was back. She was accompanied by a uniformed chauffeur, a gardener and a groom.

The groom, who was English, stated the case. "Come now, me lad," he began. "Be off with you. This is a private beach. There's plenty of shore for you natives to clutter up, what?"

"Go ahead and eject me," requested Cobb.

"If you will have it." The groom bent to grasp him by the shoulders. A pair of powerful arms lifted, drove his chin into his breast, doubled him, and sent him rolling like a ball along the strand.

THERE FOLLOWED A brief but exciting mix-up. The brown arms of Steve Cobb worked like pistons. His strong legs bounced him back and forth and in and out, and he ducked, blocked, countered and delivered powerful blows which played havoc with the groom, the gardener and the chauffeur.

Before the horrified eyes of the young mistress, the servants went down, got up, and finally remained down. Not having been engaged as pugilists, their hearts had not been in their work.

When it was all over, Steve Cobb advanced upon the girl who stood her ground but trembled. He wasn't even breathing heavily.

"Have you any more servants?" he asked blandly.

"Oh!" she exclaimed. She swung her right arm and slapped him smartly on the left cheek.

Steve laughed delightedly, pounced on her, picked her up kicking and writhing but no screaming, hugged her to his breast and kissed her leisurely.

Finally he set her on her feet. "I usually leave about this time," he said. "The sun is going down. Good afternoon."

"I'll have you horse-whipped," she flung after him.

"If you're on the beach tomorrow, I'll give you another kiss," he promised.

He walked slowly down the beach, grinning to see the beaten servants slinking back toward the big house. The girl stood like a statue where he had left her.

By and by he passed through the straggling village street and presently came to his domicile. It was an unpainted structure. There was only one window and one door, but the door had a step. On the step was sitting a young girl, maybe fifteen, but so elfin that she didn't look that old.

"Hello, Myra," he said. "What do you want to borrow this time?"

She blushed crimson. "Our hens ain't laying, Steve," she said. "Mother wondered if you had a couple of eggs."

"By a strange coincidence I have a couple of eggs, kid," he stated.

She rubbed her knuckles against her eyes.

"Oh, Steve," she wailed, "I hate to be borrowing all the time. It isn't as if we ever paid back. We're so damn shiftless."

He laughed. "Move over," he said. "Myra, I just met a princess. She was a most haughty princess who ordered a pauper off her private beach. When he wouldn't go, she summoned her entourage—make a note of that word—write a story round it and you'll get big money—so he knocked the blocks off the retinue, and then he kissed the princess and came home to find a queen sitting on his doorstep."

"Didn't you know that the Cobb Estate was occupied?" she demanded. "Are they actually closing the beach?"

"No, to the first and yes to the second, your majesty."

She sighed. "Don't it make you feel terrible, Steve, to have people living in your old home and ordering you off your beach?"

"Not at all. Like Buddha, I find that man needs no possessions to be happy."

"I wish you'd snap out of it," she said mournfully. "A fine big man like you with so much brains and you're turning into a bum. Like us."

"Myra, I wouldn't swap you for that princess with all her wealth and wardrobe. Your bare tootsies look beautiful to me."

"Don't kid me, Steve. Is she very beautiful?"

"Beauty is skin deep. She has a nasty disposition."

"Wouldn't it be fun if you married her and got your old home back?"

"Marriage, your majesty, means children. As you and I are both agreed that people would be much better off if they never have been born, it would be obviously unfair to bring children into the world. And that girl looks to me as if she would have loads of kids just for spite."

"Myra," called a shrill voice from the end of the lane. "Hurry up."

Patting the child on top of the head, he entered the hut and returned with two eggs.

"Scram, your majesty," he said, smiling. "Tell your mother to make judicious use of these."

"You big nut," she retorted, giggling. Steve went into his residence and closed the door.

It was a one room shack. A crazy stove in one corner, a table, an old sofa with torn upholstery, two wooden chairs, and a rag carpet comprised its furnishings. Steve loved it. He liked to prepare his own meals and he was a decent cook. When the weather was fair he slept on the sand under the stars.

When it rained he made shift with the sofa.

"I shouldn't have kissed that witch," he remarked as he seated himself at his evening meal. "Poisoned lips. Which describes her. Wonder who the heck she is."

2

A CONTENTED MAN

AFTER DINNER STEVE lighted his kerosene lamp, picked up his one book which was *Alice in Wonderland*, opened it in the middle and began to read aloud. He could have closed the book and gone on without missing a word, having read *Alice* at least a hundred times. Half an hour passed when he heard voices outside his door.

"Yes, sir, this is where he lives," said Myra. "And he's sitting in there reading *Alice in Wonderland*, same as he always does."

"The poor nut," said a male voice which caused Steve to scowl, not at the expletive but because he recognized the voice.

"Come on in, damn you," he shouted. "Let's have it over with."

There entered a fat man, middle-aged, bald, red faced, and smiling triumphantly.

"Run you down," he declared. "Where does a fellow sit in this pig sty?"

"All this place needed to be what you called it was you, Pennypacker," replied the host with a chuckle. "Sit on the sofa, you're better upholstered than it is. Or try that wooden chair beside the stove."

Mr. Pennypacker selected the chair. "Living in squalor," he sneered.

"Neat as wax and clean as a pin. Not squalid. You don't have to spend the week-end."

Pennypacker frowned. "What's the matter with you? Quitter?"

"I was reading a very interesting book, *Alice in Wonderland.* I hate being interrupted."

"Do you know I've been looking for you for months?"

"I've been here for six weeks. Punk detective, you are."

"Steve, I want to talk business."

"I don't."

"You've got to listen to me."

Steve produced a corncob pipe, pulled a tobacco pouch from the table drawer, filled his pipe and lighted it.

"Okay," he said pleasantly. "I'll listen."

"What's the sense of this sort of thing?"

"Suits me."

"Steve, you've a big future in business. With your record—"

Steve chuckled. "Did you ever consider the South Sea island savage, Henry?"

"Certainly I haven't."

"He's no fool. In my humble way I imitate him. I don't spend three dollars a week."

"You ass, you can make a thousand a week."

"I doubt that, but it would be at the expense of my health and tranquility. This is the life, old man. You ought to drop everything and join me. A few hours of healthful labor and I have fresh fish, oysters, clams, lobsters. By spending a few cents I can buy a steak. No clothes problem because I don't

wear any. I pay no rent. I
swim, row, run and loaf.
I sleep like a baby. I have
no nerves. And intelli-
gent companionship?
There is a friend of mine
who is a hundred and
one years old and who
is a philosopher. Would
you like to meet him?"

"You're laying down
because Rosalie Forbes
jilted you."

Steve Cobb

"On the contrary," Steve said, smiling broadly. "Rosalie
made me do everything that I didn't want to do. Tail coats,
for instance. And she kept men up until four A.M. And she
made me dance. Why should a man dance, Henry?"

"This is a pose," sneered Pennypacker.

"I'm being natural for the first time in my life. Want to
feel my muscle, Henry?"

"No, you jackass. You were strong as an elephant in
college. Don't credit your sojourn here with that."

"Well, anyway, I like it here."

"It isn't as if you were broke. You have the Cobb
Company six percent bonds, haven't you?"

Steve grinned. "You bet you. I'm sure of fifteen hundred
a year. A man can be a king on fifteen hundred a year."

"Warburton will buy them and pay big money for them."

"No doubt. He can't have them."

"Their face value is twenty-five thousand. I can get you
a hundred thousand."

Steve yawned in his face. "It's getting close to bed time. I'm up with the birds. Were you ever up with the birds, Henry?"

"With a hundred thousand you can get back into the game. Don't lay down, Steve."

"I love to lay down," Steve replied with a bland smile.

"I've been looking up the law," said Pennypacker. "I think the peculiar features of that bond issue can be set aside by the courts, but Warburton is willing to pay a good price for it."

"Oh, yeah?"

"ETHICALLY YOU HAD no business to hold out those bonds, Steve. The settlement with the Warburton interests required that your father's estate be turned over. The bonds were not included in the list through an oversight. They had been issued so many years ago that they were overlooked."

"What sort of ethics did Warburton use when he blackjacked my poor old man and picked his pockets? There was dirty work at the cross roads, Henry, and I'm not at all sure that your hands are clean—"

"Damn you," shouted Pennypacker. "I did all in my power to protect your father. He was over-extended and the depression—"

"And this wolf of a promoter, Warburton—I know. I'm not interested in business. Did you ever dig a mess of clams and make your own chowder?"

"Bah! What's your game? Warburton owns the Cobb Company lock, stock and barrel."

"Thanks to my poor old father's heart attack. If he had lived we'd have beaten that hyena. I'm damn suspicious of that heart attack, Henry."

"Pshaw. You know the strain he had been under. Point is you can't hold up Warburton. Your father's issues of stock are a precedent and if you brought suit, you'd only get the face value of the bonds. I tell you I've looked into the thing."

Lucinda Warburton

"You're Warburton's man, now, eh?"

"A lawyer must have clients," said Pennypacker with some embarrassment. "What do you plan to do?"

"Nothing. Nothing whatever."

The lawyer gazed searchingly at him. "You're deep, but don't overplay your hand. Sell for a good price—a hundred fifty thousand, maybe."

Steve laughed pleasantly. "Just tell Warburton when you get back to New York not to forget to pay the interest on the bonds."

"New York? Don't you know he's here? He moved into the Cobb mansion today. He took it with the other Cobb assets."

Steve laughed loudly. "I bet he has a daughter," he remarked.

"A lovely girl. You'll meet her. Warburton wants to be friendly."

"Humph. How did you locate me?"

Henry grinned. "Miss Warburton came home with a tale of a savage on the beach who beat up three servants. Not knowing anybody else capable of such a feat, it occurred to me that you might have returned to Cobbport."

"Well," said Steve, rising. "Go fill your lungs with sweet air. Go before I chuck you out. Don't tell Warburton I'm here. I'm snubbing the Warburtons."

Pennypacker rose. "Steve," he said uncomfortably, "Warburton is a big man, one who is accustomed to having his own way and I suspect he is not too scrupulous."

"Are you telling me?" jeered Steve.

"What I mean is that you are broke, aside from the bonds. He thinks you double-crossed him in holding them out."

"My father made me a present of them when I was twenty-one and told, me never to let go of them. They were not among his or the company's assets."

"Yes, but the fact that they were not mentioned among the company obligations—"

"Why should they have been? Father was dead. Blame the book-keeping department."

"Yes, but while it's doubtful if you can use them to block his plans, their existence is a menace. If you don't do business with him, you may regret it."

Steve stretched out his arms, shut his fists, drew in his forearms and gazed complacently at his biceps.

"Perhaps I did need an interest in life," he observed. "Well, well, well, something might drop on me. Good night, Henry. Pleasant dreams."

3

STEVE SNUBS A MILLIONAIRE

ABOUT THREE THE following afternoon Stephen Cobb was lying on the beach, semi-nude as usual, with his battered straw hat over his eyes, his arms spread out and his abdomen rising and falling with the regularity of slumber.

His location, however, was not in front of the Cobb estate but a quarter of a mile below where the sand was less soft and where there were piles of pebbles.

"So," said a voice with an edge to it. "So this is where you are."

Steve pushed the hat away and gazed up at her.

"You are getting to be a pest," he remarked.

"So you were afraid," she said contemptuously.

"So you took off the pants and put on a skirt," he commented. "Well, it's an improvement, but, even so, I don't like you."

"No?" She laughed lightly. "You asserted you would sleep on my beach this afternoon. And you were afraid."

He grinned at her. "I decided to snub you."

"You said you were going to kiss me again," she reminded him maliciously. "Well?"

"I don't seem to want to."

She drew from behind her back a riding crop.

"How fortunate," she said coldly.

His right hand darted out, grasped a slender ankle, and toppled the girl upon the sand. He rolled her over, secured the riding crop, and sent it flying into the water. He placed his face within a few inches of hers and gazed sternly into her eyes.

"You don't tempt me," he said brutally. "Go home."

Releasing her he resumed his reclining position but his hands were behind his head.

She sat up slowly. Her pretty little face was crimson and her eyes blazing.

"Why did you kiss me yesterday if I didn't tempt you?" she asked through clenched teeth.

"I thought it would make you mad. Go home."

She locked her hands and placed them around bent knees.

"Nevertheless, you were afraid to return to my beach."

"Okay. I was afraid," he said indifferently.

She cocked her head on one side. "You weren't. There was some other reason. You are a very nasty brute but I'd like to know the reason."

"Very well. I don't care to continue our acquaintance."

The girl leaped indignantly to her feet. "Acquaintance? I ordered a dirty beachcomber from my property and he talks of acquaintance! Oh, if I had my whip!"

"Just a minute."

The receding tide had left the whip on the water's edge. He retrieved it and handed it to her.

"Lay on, Simon Legree," he said cheerfully. "See if you can make me holler."

She fingered it wistfully. "It would serve you right," she

said in a voice which shook with anger. "Why are you so nasty?"

"I hate women. I hate blondes, brunettes and red-headed ones. I hate women who have private beaches. The prettier they are the more I hate them."

"Then you think I'm pretty?" she asked eagerly.

"Yes, but bad tempered. Would it make you wildly angry if I kissed you?"

"It certainly would."

"I don't believe you. You've spoiled my nap and I'm going home."

With that he turned his back to her and walked swiftly away.

She stood there on the beach gazing furiously after him.

"I'm going to have trouble with that girl," he said solemnly.

THERE WAS AN expensive touring car standing in front of the post office of Cobbport's single business street. It was a gaudy foreign machine with an incredibly long and shiny hood and a dozen loafers were gravely inspecting it. Steve noticed the spruceness of the liveried chauffeur and observed an elderly man who stood in the post office door-way chatting with Silas Cobb, the postmaster.

"Oh, Steve," the postmaster called. "This gentleman was asking about you. It's Mr. Warburton who—er—bought the Cobb estate."

Steve nodded and continued on his way. He had never seen Warburton but the fellow resembled his newspaper pictures. He was a smartly dressed, old young man with pink cheeks, very white hair, and a white mustache waxed at the corners. He had a large predatory nose and a large tightly clamped mouth and he resembled very little the young woman who had gone looking for a young beach-comber with a riding crop clutched tightly in her hand.

Five minutes' walk brought him to the narrow lane at the left which led to what Pennypacker had described, not inaptly, as a pig sty.

As he made to turn he was overtaken by the foreign car.

"Oh, Mr. Cobb, a moment please." Warburton had a harsh imperative note in his bass voice which grated upon the young man.

"Sorry, I'm in a hurry," he flung over his shoulder.

He heard the door of the car open and shut and foot-steps behind him.

"My dear Mr. Cobb, a moment, please."

Steve waited for him. They contrasted strangely, the millionaire in his English blazer and panama hat and white flannels, and Cobb in his bathing shorts and burnished copper skin.

"Well, sir," Steve said gruffly.

"I have only just learned that we are neighbors. You know of course who I am."

"I've heard of you."

Warburton's cheeks grew pinker. "No hard feelings, I hope," he said hurriedly. "It was the fortunes of war, young man."

"You took a great load off my shoulders and my mind," replied Steve with a half smile. "No very hard feelings."

"Well, well, well, I thought by your manner, you didn't want to meet me."

"I didn't. I'm tired of your kind of people."

"Ah, you are bitter."

"You are gazing, Mr. Warburton, upon a happy man. I wouldn't change places with you if—if you gave me that purple blazer with the brass buttons."

Warburton laughed politely. "Naturally. You have youth. I am old. Mr. Cobb, I wish to tell you that you are a remarkable sales manager. That trans-continental trip of yours brought wonderful results considering the depression. I had heavier artillery than your father—"

"Pardon me, sir, but I came down here to escape business."

"And so did I," declared Warburton heartily. "Let's not discuss it. I feel sensitive about occupying your old home. I want to tell you that you will be a welcome guest. I want you to meet my family."

"Thanks, but I'm not going out this season, Mr. Warburton."

"Come, come, my boy. Look here. How would you like to be sales manager of the reorganized Cobb Company?"

"I'd hate it."

"Well, well. You *are* bitter. What can I do?"

"Let me alone, please," said Steve. "And good afternoon."

Leaving the affronted millionaire standing in the lane, Steve Cobb padded swiftly in his bare feet to his cabin, entered and threw himself on the couch.

"Phew!" he exclaimed. "The place smells of Warburton's."

He climbed on a chair and lifted from its hiding place on one of the rafters a paper shoe box which he opened and drew forth a package of engraved certificates. These were gold bonds of the Cobb Concrete Company, issued in 1914 and had ten years to run.

These bonds were a lien upon the property, a first mortgage with plenary powers. At the time of issue, the company had been a small affair which since had grown enormously. Its over expansion was the cause of its wreckage. There were clauses in these bonds seriously hampering financing operations, so fifteen years before Steve's father had bought them in and placed them in trust for his son. When Warburton had beaten the company's stock and more recent issues of bonds down to almost nothing and then acquired the company, incidentally breaking its founder's heart, it was probable that he knew nothing of this original bond issue.

No amount of money would buy them. They were a hair inside Warburton's shirt, a thorn in his crown, a nail in his shoe. So the game was to coddle Steve and make a fuss over him and persuade him to sell.

4

DECLARATION OF WAR

STEVE WAS DIGGING himself a mess of clams about ten the following morning when Miss Warburton appeared on the scene. She was wearing a costume of white flannel. She had on high heeled French shoes and a walking staff was in her hand. Her hair was like an aureole and her eyes were bright and she smiled at him from afar.

"Hold everything," he said to himself. "Circe advances."

"Hello," she called.

"Mornin'," he said grumpily.

"I am full of apologies, Mr. Cobb," she informed him.

"Forget it, Miss Warburton."

She came close and watched him as he thrust his spade into the sand. It came up with much mud and a couple of sizable clams.

"Father told me who you were, last night. Why didn't you come to dinner? On account of me?"

"I don't like French chefs."

"Oh! I feel dreadful about ordering you off your own beach. And living in your house. Perhaps I'm in your room. Which was your room?"

"I'm sorry I kissed you, since you're sorry you set the menials on me."

"Oh, that isn't exactly complimentary."

"I don't think anything of kissing a girl," stated Steve. "Forget it."

She placed her little hands on her hips and lifted her chin.

"You are a great hulking clod," she said vindictively. "A mass of flesh and bones. You have the mentality of a third rate prize fighter. You must have been absurd as a business man. No wonder you couldn't protect your property. You are right where you belong—digging clams."

His face reddened but he managed a laugh.

"Not worth bothering about," he remarked. "Well, Miss Warburton, I used to know a lot of girls of your type. Like a fool I got engaged to one. Neurotic, unprincipled, mercenary little monkeys. I suppose your father told you to be nice to me. Well, I don't like your father. I don't care much for you."

"Liar," she snapped. "You liked kissing me. I could tell."

"I did it to infuriate you. I hated it. Now will you go away?"

He bent over his spade or he might have been alarmed by the rage in her eyes.

"I'll go," she said. "I'll make you crawl on the ground. I'll make you grovel. Oh, I'll grind you under my heel."

"If you're here in one second," he said without looking up, "I'll lay you across my knee."

He heard a scuffling of sand as Miss Warburton departed in a hurry.

"If I liked girls," he remarked aloud, "I'd go for that one. Spunky little brat."

At the end of an hour, having filled a pail with clams, he suspended mining operations and became aware that a green yawl had slipped into the bay and was letting go her anchor. It was a fifty footer, broad of beam and seaworthy.

"You could go round the world in her," he commented. "Wonder what brought her into this jumping-off place. Well, what the heck do I care?"

After that he strolled, pail in hand and spade on shoulder, back to the village. That the green yawl was going to have an influence upon his life, he had no premonition.

COBBPORT LAYS ON the south side of the Cape. Except for one hundred yards-on the Cobb estate, in fact, comprises all that is beautiful and desirable in Cobbport, a peninsula shaped like a crescent, about half a mile long, which forms the little harbor.

The original Cobb, Ezra by name, bought the peninsula away back in the year 1700, when peninsulas were to be had for little or nothing. The village was a straggling affair, at least half of whose inhabitants were descendants of the original Cobb. Those who were not Cobbs were named Sears or Bearce or Burton.

They were folks without ambition who, as a result of generations of sea food augmented by salt pork were stringy, anæmic and shiftless.

Ezra Cobb, Steve's grandfather, had been different. He had gone to New York, plunged into business, made a fortune for his time, and, never having forgotten Cobbport, had returned, built a huge house to replace the cottage on his property and lived there for three months in the year.

When he died, it was found that his wealth had dwindled, but his son, Ezra, Junior, had inherited his business enterprise, and soon repaired the family fortunes.

Steve's father had vision. His business had grown by

leaps and bounds. It had grown so large that it attracted the attention of a big bad wolf of Wall Street named Warburton. The chicanery of Mr. Warburton in conjunction with the depression had licked Ezra Cobb. Despite the tremendous energy of his son, Steve, he had gone to the wall and everything he owned had gone with him.

And now, by some whim, Warburton was living on the Cobb estate with a young wife and a twenty-year-old daughter, while Steve Cobb seemed to have revested to the status of his various distant relatives who had never ventured out of Cobbport.

While the Cobb mansion was old-fashioned, it was spacious and exceedingly comfortable. There were fifteen master's bedrooms, six servants' rooms, a huge stable which had been turned into a garage, store houses, hot houses, and a wonderful garden. From every room in the house there was a gorgeous view of the sea.

When Steve returned to the village there was muttering up and down Main Street. From time immemorial the natives had been privileged to use Cobb's bathing beach and to picnic on the Cobb grounds. Workmen were running a wall across the base of the peninsula and cutting off the beach with a wire fence.

Josh Sears stopped Steve to ask if tradition hadn't given Cobbport folks a legal right to overrun the beach and grounds.

Steve shook his head. "My father took steps to prevent 'right of way' many years ago," he said. "His lawyers took care of it. About all you can do is overcharge Warburton for everything he buys in town."

"And don't you think we won't," declared Mr. Sears, who owned the general store.

5

THE "TROUBLE MAN"

THREE NIGHTS AFTER Miss Warburton had come upon Steve Cobb digging clams, William Warburton was sitting in the Cobb library with a person who had come down from New York.

This was a curious-looking person. He was very tall and he had no back to his head. He had protruding ears and pits on his face which indicated that he had had smallpox in his youth. He had small greenish eyes and a long narrow chin and a very large mouthful of irregular teeth. As his upper lip was short, when he smiled he revealed a half inch of unhealthy looking gum. Although he was wearing a tuxedo which fitted him, he was obviously no gentleman.

His name was Hutton and he was Warburton's trouble man. When Warburton had trouble getting something honestly, he sent for Hutton. He never asked Hutton questions which might embarrass Warburton. As the man was bound to him—Warburton could hang him—he talked to him more freely and frankly than to any other human being.

Warburton, who came of a good Maryland family with gentlemanly ancestors and was rightfully in the Blue Book of New York, and who had inherited a large fortune and built it into an enormous one, both despised and admired Hutton. He had summoned him as soon as he learned that Stephen Cobb was his neighbor.

"When I took over the Cobb Company," he explained, "I discovered a most annoying situation. In order to get started, Cobb issued twenty-five thousand dollars' worth of bonds through a bank in Worcester, Massachusetts. These bonds had amazing restrictions. For example they limit capitalization. In fact, Cobb's various issues of new stock were in violation of the bond agreement."

"Why didn't the bond holders stop them?"

"Because Cobb was shrewd enough to buy them in within a few years after starting the business."

"Then he retired them."

"No. Instead, he gave them to his son. If we had known about their existence, we could have forced young Cobb to disgorge when the control of the company came into our hands. You see they were not listed and had never been sold over the counter and their existence had been forgotten. Cobb put out six different issues of stock in twenty years."

"The Yankee crook."

"No, the fool was honest. If he hadn't died suddenly, he would probably have thrown these bonds on the table. As things were, we took over and had begun the work of reorganization when our auditor discovered that the bonds had never been retired. He then dug up the terms on which they had been issued. The owner of those bonds can block every move, Hutton. The company was originally capitalized at a hundred thousand. Cobb expanded it to ten million. In order to make a profit I've got to turn it into a twenty-five million corporation. Instead, there never was a legal right to increase capitalization beyond a hundred thousand. The company is liable for all dividends paid on stock illegally issued. I can't put out the new stock until those bonds are retired."

"You say this boy is living here in a hut and has no money at all?"

"Right."

"Well, buy the bonds from him."

"I sent Pennypacker to see him. He won't sell."

"He'll sell if you pay him enough." Warburton shook his head. "I'll lose the five millions I've sunk in this company if I can't put out new stock. I called on him myself the other day."

"What's his game?"

"He's no fool. He knows that we—er—violated ethics—"

"Ethics?" Hutton laughed heartily. "We busted the whole ten commandments."

"I fear he bears malice."

"Maybe he heard something."

"Pennypacker says no. He has no suspicion. But it galls him to think the company has passed out of his family. He is biding his time."

"LISTEN, IF HE tips over the apple-cart, he shows up his old man as a crook."

"Hardly. As Cobb had the entire issue of bonds in his possession, he had a right to run his business as he pleased. But this boy can block my every move. He can hold me up. Hutton, there are millions at stake!"

"I'm getting sick of doing your dirty work, Warburton," said Hutton with a scowl.

"I would like those bonds, please," said the millionaire coldly.

"Are they registered?"

"Never were registered."

"Records of paying interest to Stephen Cobb, though."

"The last coupon was paid six months ago. We took over the company

Warburton

two weeks later. It could be arranged as though the bonds had come to us in the settlement of Cobb's affairs as this estate came into my hands; partial payment of Ezra Cobb's obligations to me."

"If this young fellow happened to be found dead, you mean?"

"Hutton, I forbid you to talk in such a manner," said Warburton, flushing angrily.

"Well, if you could get the bonds, and Steve Cobb sort of vanished, you could turn them over to the treasurer for retirement, show a canceled check for payment—"

"No need for that. As it is a small total, payment could have been made in cash. Or, better still, have the bonds appear on the list of Cobb assets turned over to me as of six months ago."

"The bonds are in a safety deposit vault?"

"No. Six weeks ago, he gave up his vault in the City National in New York and came directly to Cape Cod. There is no bank in this town. I suspect he keeps them near him. You see, I found out about the bonds and immediately started to keep tabs on the fellow. Why do you suppose I moved into this old ark in this down-at-the-heels summer resort?"

Hutton smiled nastily. "You figured you had a couple of vamps to sic on him. Which one were you going to use, your daughter or her stepmother?"

Warburton seized a paper weight and lifted it menacingly.

Hutton drew an automatic from his pocket and leveled it at his employer.

"I'd sooner shoot you than anybody I know," he said in a very low tone, which was almost a hiss. "I know you, Warburton. You'd use either of them if there was dough in it. You're meaner than a hyena and dirtier than a snake. So he won't fall for dames, eh?"

WARBURTON, VERY PALE, set down the paper weight. "Put away that weapon," he snarled.

"You dare not use it."

"Some day, when I get a little sicker of living, I may," replied Hutton. "I'm rotten, but not in your class."

"Damn you," cried Warburton, who was like a ghost.

"Let it pass. I get fifty thousand if the bonds come back in a way to do you some good."

Warburton, with an effort, recovered. "I could send you to the chair," he said significantly.

"Yes, but I could make things hot for you. Fifty thousand." Warburton nodded.

There was a knock on the door. "May I come in?" asked a woman with a peculiarly vibrant voice.

"Come in, my dear," he called loudly. He was eager to conclude the interview.

There entered a woman so beautiful and so striking that Hutton, the trouble man, drew in his breath sharply and even Warburton's jaded eyes kindled.

She was tall, with an enchanting figure. She had jet black hair braided and dressed in such a way as to make her appear to be wearing a crown of ebony. Her skin was the color of yellow ivory, clear, softly glowing, smooth as satin. She wore a black silk evening dress cut very low. Her arms were marvelous, her neck and shoulders rarely beautiful.

Her small head was regally held and her great black eyes were absolutely gorgeous. She had a small straight nose and a small mouth with very full lips. She smiled politely at Hutton, but her eyes did not smile. There was something enigmatic about her face. It was beautiful as a siren's is beautiful and about it there was something not exactly wholesome. She looked like a woman who has seen much and felt little, and took much and given nothing. She had been married to Warburton for five years and scorned him. He hated her and continued to be fascinated by her.

"Well, well, my dear," he said fussily. "We've just concluded our conference."

She turned her eyes on Hutton. "Bird of ill omen," she said in that curiously haunting voice of hers, "what agony have you and my dear husband been preparing for someone?"

"Just a business conference," said Hutton uncomfortably. "I'm sure you and your husband want to bill and coo, so if you'll excuse me, I'll be driving over to Hyannis."

"Aren't you staying here?" she asked mockingly. Hutton had never been a guest in any of Warburton's houses.

"No, Mrs. Warburton. Not this time," he said. "Good night."

Mrs. Warburton sank gracefully into a big chair by the fireplace.

"William," she said in a tone which always infuriated him, "I saw the most beautiful man this afternoon. He was half naked. He has the torso of a god. Such arms! Such bulging muscles! Such legs! A chest on which I longed to lay my head. And a magnificent head, like a shaved Viking, though his hair was brown, not golden. I gazed at him in rapture. I am afraid I was mentally unfaithful, my dear."

"You are a vicious woman," said Warburton darkly. "I'm damned if I know why I ever married you."

"I know why I married you, darling. For your money. What else have you to offer, pray?" she said insolently. "This boy—I don't suppose he is more than twenty-five, carried a pail full of clams and over his right shoulder was a spade. He walked with the grace of Apollo. Do you know, I felt like asking him if I might carry his pail. I would like to be the squaw of that young savage."

Warburton rose and stood over her. "I would like very much to strangle you," he growled.

"Darling," she cried. She leaped up and threw her arms around his neck, kissed him passionately upon the lips and, when he made to embrace her, she ran out of the room laughing wildly.

He called her an unpublishable name. A thousand times during the past five years he had vowed to divorce this artist's model whom he had married in haste and who had tortured him ever since.

6

THE AFFAIR AT THE HUT

THE INDIFFERENCE OF Stephen Cobb to wealth, women and other good things of life was far from being a pose. He had been reared like most rich men's sons. After graduating from Harvard, he had gone into the business with no notion that conditions were going to grab him and make a slave out of him. He had plenty of money and lots of playtime, at first. During this period he had met and fallen in love with Rosalie Forbes, a beautiful, gay young woman who desired to marry a rich and handsome husband.

The depression had caught Ezra Cobb with his business unsafely expanded. For some years it had boomed and its owner, instead of piling up a surplus for emergencies, had used profits to build new factories and increase output.

Steve, who had served an apprenticeship as a salesman, had been made sales manager shortly after the depression. For years he had worked ten or twelve hours a day at his desk and had been dragged around at night by Rosalie, who was insatiable in her desire for excitement.

He had worked terrifically and fought a losing fight. The securities of the company dropped steadily and business faded even more rapidly. In desperation he started on a tour of the country in search of new business and he was so successful that he might have pulled the company through, if William Warburton had not taken advantage of his father's financial stress to wrest the control of the company from his nerveless fingers.

While Steve was in California news had come of his father's sudden death. As he was leaving for the east there had come a wire from Warburton offering him the post of sales manager. This he hadn't troubled to answer.

Having a majority of the voting stock, Warburton closed down all the plants of the company throwing thousands out of work and picked up stocks and several bond issues at his own price. The structure Ezra Cobb had raised was shattered; his private fortune which Steve was supposed to have inherited had gone into the pot, and all that was left to the son and heir was the small original issue of bonds, the curious character of which Steve was unaware at the time.

His father had put them in trust for him when he was under age and he had not perused them when they came into his possession. All he remembered about them was that Ezra had a queer smile on his face when he told him about the trust. "Never let go of them.

"They may come in very useful sometime, son."

A plane had landed him in New York in time for his father's funeral. Rosalie had walked down the aisle on his arm and had given him back his ring the following night.

He didn't care. He was so tired he didn't care about anything. For a few months he had lived at his club until the cash in his possession was almost gone and then he had begun to yearn for the Cape, with its scrub pines and its salt breezes and the softness of the air from the gulf stream.

And in three months Steve Cobb had reverted to type—

almost. He had traveled on his nerve for years. He had been worried sick most of the time. Here he had found peace. Here he was content.

He could have lived fairly well for a small sum on the Cape, but he preferred to live like a savage in a hut. He had lost his ambition. Knowing that Warburton had secured the Cobb Company by sharp practice and chicanery he didn't care. Someday, if he felt the urge, he might make things unpleasant for Warburton, but there was no hurry. Hurry was stupid.

On this particular night it was very warm. He sat outside talking to Myra Sears until ten o'clock. Myra was a sweet child. Her father was totally worthless, her mother a worried haggard woman, old before her time.

Myra was going to high school and she wanted to go to college. Steve had a notion that, by the time she was ready for college, he might snap out of his lethargy and make money enough to gratify the child's ambition. But, so far, he hadn't promised anything.

"I got to go home," the child said at ten o'clock. "Where you going to sleep tonight, Steve?"

"I think I'll climb the hummock back there and sleep in the grass," he said. "Since they cut off the beach, I've been going up there. Too many pebbles on the town beach."

"The hateful things! What harm does it do them if we use the beach?"

"Pride of property, Myra. Let's hope that you and I never get that way."

She laughed ruefully. "Gosh, I guess I'll never have any property to be proud over. Good night, Steve."

"Pleasant dreams, kid."

BY AND BY Steve took a
blanket and climbed the
hummock back of the hut.
He spread it on the long
grass about a hundred
yards from his domi-
cile and rolled himself
in it. Usually he went
immediately to sleep,
but tonight he remained
awake for a while. Being
a kind-hearted fellow, his
conscience troubled him

Mrs. Warburton

because he felt that he had been nasty to the Warburton
girl.

True, she had ordered him off the beach and brought
down three servants to drive him away, but he had been
insolent and had goaded her into doing that.

He had forcibly kissed her, after beating up the lackeys,
so the next day she had come after him, when she found
her own beach vacant, carrying the riding crop in case he
kissed her again. That meant she rather hoped he would
and she probably would not have used the riding crop. The
least he could have done was to have accommodated her
when he had overpowered her.

And the other day when she had come to him full of
good will because she had learned he wasn't a common
peasant but her own kind of people, he had been especially
disagreeable. After all, it wasn't her fault that Warburton
was her father. And she was very good looking and rather
gallant.

After sleeping for an hour or two, he was awakened by a tug at the blanket. He opened his eyes. There was no moon, but the stars gave light enough to enable him to recognize the strained anxious face of Myra Sears.

"Listen, brat," he said reprovingly, "ladies should never go into a man's bedchamber."

She giggled. "This is outdoors and it's all right," she informed him. "Steve, I couldn't sleep tonight, somehow, and I can see out the window down to your house from my bed and there's a light moving round in your house."

Steve sat up. "That's a good one! Robbing my shack," he said chuckling. "Why didn't they pick Warburton's? I wish 'em joy of what they find there. Good God!"

"What's the matter?"

"You go home."

He rose and went swiftly down the little hill and approached his hut from the rear. There was no window at the rear or on the sides, but there were chinks in the boards and he saw a glimmer of light.

Noiselessly he sped around the house.

A blanket served as a curtain for the window and it didn't quite reach the sill. Steve applied his eye.

THERE WAS A man sitting at the table within who was inspecting, by the aid of a flashlight, a package of engraved paper. At his elbow was a cardboard shoe box. Within reach of his right hand was an automatic pistol. On the muzzle of the pistol was a jigger which Steve judged to be a silencer.

He moved noiselessly to the door. It was not fastened because it possessed neither lock or bolt. He pushed it open, stood for a second in the doorframe and dropped flat.

The intruder had turned his light on the door-frame, picked up his pistol and fired as Steve dropped.

There were four almost simultaneous reports so smothered that they were almost inaudible; four flashes and four pinging sounds as the bullets went out of doors.

Steve lay flat. He heard the chair pushed back. A couple of steps and the man stood over him. He turned the flashlight upon the naked back. His right hand, holding the pistol, dangled at his side.

Suddenly the weapon was torn from his hand, a bullet escaping as he pressed the trigger. A heavy weight rolled against his legs, and he crashed down upon the old and creaking floor. And then a pair of hands were at his throat. He kicked, he twisted and squirmed, but the iron hands tightened. He grew limp. Life seemed to go out of him. Steve rose, went to the table, lit the lamp, replaced the bonds in the box, laid the pistol on the table, took a chair, stood on it and replaced the box upon the rafter. As he did so he heard a scraping noise. He leaped to the floor as the robber, who had recovered during Steve's leisurely movements and had crawled to the table, rose up to grasp his weapon.

As head and arm came above the level of the table, a huge right fist crashed against his left temple. The man went backwards and down with a leaden thud and lay still.

"Naughty, naughty," chided Steve Cobb. "I'll have to find another hiding place for these bonds."

He drew water in a tin dipper and dumped it upon the man's face. The fellow didn't move. Alarmed, Steve dropped on hands and knees beside him and placed his hand on the heart. He felt no beat. He laid his ear against the robber's chest. The heart had ceased to beat.

7

COMMITTED TO THE DEEP

"I KILLED HIM," murmured Steve. "God in heaven, I've killed him!" He blew out the light, groped for a chair and sat down heavily.

And suddenly a still small voice was heard.

"Who was there, Steve?" asked Myra.

"No one. If there was a robber he was gone. Go to bed."

"I saw lights," she persisted. "Can I come in?"

"Certainly not—at this hour. Go home like a nice child."

"Did he steal anything?"

"What is there to steal?"

"That's right. Well, good night, Steve."

"Good night, Myra," he said absently.

He sat there with clenched fists for several minutes. The dead man was unknown to him, but of course he was an emissary of Warburton's. What had made Warburton think he would keep bonds in the shack? It didn't matter. There was a dead man here and what was to be done about it?

A man has a right to defend his home. The intruder had fired four shots before he had been overpowered. A jury would not convict; not a Cape Cod jury loyal to its own people and hating the rich summer folks. Only there was no way of bringing Warburton into it.

Steve closed the door and again lighted his lamp. He went on his knees beside the body and studied the face. An ugly individual but very well dressed. He thrust his hand into the breast pocket of the coat. He pulled forth a flat wallet which he opened. It contained thirty or forty dollars in cash and several visiting cards, all of which bore the name of Frank P. Hutton.

Ah! thought Steve. Hutton, the trouble man! He had heard of him. Hutton was responsible for the strike at the Elmira plant. Hutton was supposed to have caused sabotage at Weston.

Ezra Cobb had told his son that Hutton was one of the biggest scoundrels alive and that he did all the dirty work for Warburton.

Steve's conscience ceased to trouble him.

It was clear enough now. Pennypacker, who was playing both sides against the middle, had been sent to sound out Steve regarding a sale of the bonds. Reporting that there was no chance of a sale, he had departed and Warburton had tried his hand at establishing friendly relations, had even told his daughter to be nice to the clam digger. And, being rebuffed on all sides, he had sent for the trouble man.

What should he do? Wake up the constable and tell his tale? It would mean an inquest, perhaps he might be held for trial.

There was no question that Hutton had come to steal the bonds and to murder their owner. They would be useless with Steve Cobb alive to claim theft and to prove ownership. The trust company could testify that they had been delivered to him on his twenty-first birthday. There was no mention of them in his father's settlement with Warburton. But, if Steve were dead, Warburton could retire the bonds as of six months past, and there would be no one to object.

So Hutton had intended to murder Steve Cobb. And Warburton had sent him to commit the double crime.

Steve smiled grimly. Let Warburton wonder what had become of his trouble man.

He picked up the corpse from the floor and flung it over his shoulder. There was terrific power in Cobb's back and shoulders. He held the intercollegiate record for weight lifting and hammer throwing and a hundred fifty pounds of dead weight on his back did not particularly inconvenience him.

Slipping round the side of the shack, he moved swiftly up to the hummock where he had been sleeping, and making a detour round the village, he reached the shore and waded into the water. Under water his burden weighed only a tenth of what it had on shore. Supporting Hutton with his left arm, he struck out with long, easy untiring strokes. Steve could swim indefinitely. While not rapid, he could travel ten miles in the water without undue fatigue.

Presently he was abreast of the peninsula on which stood his ancestral home. There were no lights in the house. Away to the left the green yawl swung at anchor and he saw several lighted portholes. He turned inshore, though there was little chance that he would be spotted from the yawl on the black water. He had proceeded but a short distance when he heard the sound of rowlocks. A boat was coming out from the landing on the peninsula above the beach. He stopped swimming, supporting Hutton easily, and waited.

It was unusual for a boat to be abroad in this quiet haven at one or two in the morning.

BY AND BY he saw the outline of the boat. It came closer and he discerned the rower—it was a woman—the silhouetted figure had to be a woman.

The boat passed and a light appeared on the deck of the yawl and he saw a shadowy figure. The rower waved an arm, and a shawl fell back and it was a naked arm.

The boat ran alongside and the woman was helped aboard the yacht. A low feminine laugh floated over the water.

"They're all alike, damn them!" he muttered. So Miss Warburton had sneaked out of her father's house to keep a nocturnal tryst on the green yawl. He had heard tales about Rosalie. Rich men's daughters were like that, apparently. No morals. No decency. To hell with them.

"Come on, Hutton," he said grimly to his ghostly companion.

Time passed and Cobb swam steadily on. He was far out in the Sound and he had farther to go. He knew when the tide would turn and how its current would sweep through the wide space between the mainland and Nantucket out into the boundless reaches of the Atlantic. Hutton was going on his last long ride. A couple of miles from shore he released him. Saw the body slowly sink and rise again. It would float of course, but that was of no consequence.

He lay on his back and gazed up at the stars as he floated on the warm water. Technically he was a murderer, but it didn't matter. A year ago this experience would have given him the jitters. Now he was placidly content. No nerves. Two miles from shore, being carried along now by the

The man went flying backwards

current, and that didn't bother him. This was the life and he loved this life.

After a few minutes, he rolled over and struck out for the shore. It was wonderful to be naked in the sea at night. Save for the narrow trunks, he was as he had been born. He had fully three miles to make homeward, though only two miles from land, because he had to work against the tide. An hour and a half.

And an hour and a half later he swam into the haven just comfortably tired. Hutton he had dismissed completely from his mind. There were lights visible on the yawl and the rowboat floated at the yacht's ladder. The little wretch was still visiting. In a year or two she would marry some poor fool.

He did not have to keep away from the yawl now and she lay directly in his course. Presently he came abreast of her and at that instant a woman lifted her voice in a scream of poignant distress.

He hesitated. "Serves her right," he muttered. "The deuce with her."

And then he remembered how she had stood on the beach looking after him, riding crop clutched in her grip, upon their second meeting. After all, she was young and, with the kind of father she had, not entirely to blame for what she was.

He turned abruptly and made for the ladder. He grasped it and pulled himself up on deck and looked around. The hatchway to the companionway was shut. No one on deck.

"No, no, no, no," the female voice cried shrilly. "For pity's sake!"

In two strides he was at the hatch, pulled open the door, and grasping the top, swung himself right into the middle of the cabin.

A woman was being forced upon a velvet bunk, protesting not only with voice, but feet and finger nails. A burly man in white flannels was bending over her.

"By God you will!" he growled.

"Tarzan!" she cried wildly, and laughed madly. "It's Tarzan come to save me."

In fact the young giant, bronzed like a savage, dripping water upon the thick carpet, his solid jaw thrust forward, his grey eyes glittering viciously, bore a certain resemblance to the hero of the movies, especially his costume.

8

THE WOMAN ON THE YAWL

THE OAF IN flannels swung about and the woman planted her feet on deck and slipped deftly away from the couch. Steve gaped at her in astonishment for he had never seen her before in his life. Not the Warburton girl. Positively not the Warburton girl. He had done her an injustice.

"You big ape, get the hell off my boat," growled the man. He was a big fellow himself and no coward. He clenched his fists.

"Why, sure," said Steve, grinning. "Sorry to spoil sport. I was passing by and thought I heard a woman cry for help."

He gazed at the cabin table upon which were the remains of a bountiful meal. There were glasses half filled with champagne, and four empty champagne bottles on the deck near a table leg.

"It's my savage!" exclaimed the woman. "Why, you wonderful creature, you did hear me cry for help."

The man pointed his arm at Steve. "Get out quick," he commanded harshly.

Steve laughed in his face. "Don't be like that," he pleaded. "I see you have caviar. It's been off my diet for months. Mind if I help myself?"

The woman laughed musically. "We'd love to have you join us," she declared. "Wouldn't we, Jack."

"I'm going to throw that brute off the boat," said the man through clenched teeth.

"If he goes, I'll go with him," she said gayly.

Steve stepped to the table, picked up a knife, and placed a huge portion of caviar on a cracker.

"I don't want to break up the party. Go right on with your fun," he said pleasantly.

The yachtsman rushed, both arms swinging.

Steve turned just in time, lifted his right leg until his knee was against his chest, drove it forth, and his large, well-formed foot planted itself against the shirt-front of the belligerent.

The man went flying backward and landed in a surprised heap against the opposite wall.

"You adorable young man!" cried the woman. "I love you for that."

Steve gazed at her curiously. She was a glowing brunette, lovely as sin. Being a little intoxicated, her lips were loose and very attractive.

"You don't look to me as if you'd object to some excitement," he said coldly. "You knew what this guy was up to. Why come out and take his caviar and champagne if you weren't going to play the game through?"

"Damned if I don't like the fellow," remarked the yachtsman who still lay, being both drunk and groggy, in his corner.

"You have a fine brand of caviar," said Steve cheerfully. "Mind if I have some more?"

The woman pulled up the strap of her black satin gown, which had dropped to her elbow in the struggle.

"Jack," she said, "I might change my mind if you would chastise this big beast."

"She's kidding you," declared Steve.

"Why, you big countryman, you don't know anything," she cried angrily.

The man named Jack rose.

"Young fellow," he said. "Take her ashore with you. She's been giving me a run around for a year. What's your name?"

"Steve Cobb!" Steve was still eating caviar with great enjoyment.

The effect of his name upon the pair would have astonished Steve if he had been looking at them. The man thrust his hand into his hip pocket. The woman made a warning gesture. Her eyes were round as apples and her cheeks whitened.

"YOU MEAN YOU are Ezra Cobb's son?" she asked shakily.

"None other," said Steve casually. "You both have the advantage of me, by the way."

"I am Mrs. William Warburton," she replied. "And this is John Clews who, besides being the owner of this yacht, is rather well known in Wall Street."

"How are you?" said Steve politely. "You know caviar is one of the things a fellow can't get fishing out of Cobbport."

"I'm sorry I called you a clamdigger," said Mrs. Warburton whose eyes continued to warn her companion.

"But I am. May I ask Mrs. Warburton if your husband knows you're out?"

"He does not," she said with a forced laugh. "If you care to tell him, I have no objections."

"Oh, I'm not speaking to your husband. I don't like him."

She laughed gayly. "Neither do I, so we have a bond in common. Come, Jack, shake hands with Mr. Cobb."

"Glad to know you," said Clews with a sour grin. "I suppose you were just passing by as you said."

"Swimming round," replied Steve.

"I suppose I'd have barged on board as you did if I'd heard Diana's howls."

"We're all friends here," said Mrs. Warburton cheerfully. "Open another bottle, Jack. A night-cap. I'm going ashore with Mr. Cobb."

"I don't drink," stated Steve, "and I'm leaving now. You might start screaming on me. Can't take chances. Good evening, folks."

Without waiting for an answer he leaped up the hatchway and a second later they heard a splash.

"Damn queer he happened to be swimming close to the yacht," observed Clews.

"Isn't he amazing," she cried enthusiastically. "Such a physique. If he had been the man, Jack, I wouldn't have screamed."

"You made a hell of a hit with him," sneered Clews. "He's a thick-headed lout. Just a swimmer."

"My husband says he was a super-salesman."

"Well, all that needs is a front and a glad hand. Everything's hunky. What say we resume from where we left off?"

"That's cold. I'm rowing ashore. I'm not quitting William until I'm sure which way the cat is going to jump."

"You're a cold-blooded witch, despite those passionate orbs of yours. Do as you please. I wonder if you've told me all the facts."

"You know all that I know. The game is in our hands."

"I'm going to look into that. It may not be. We need this fellow."

Diana Warburton smiled confidently. "I'll get him. Before I'm through with that young man I'll have a ring in his nose."

"Yeah. I'm a bit nervous about Warburton. He's a bad combination of fox and wolf."

"Losing your nerve?" she sneered.

"Before I go up against him I want four aces."

"We'll have 'em. Good night, Jack. No, no kisses. I've lost the mood."

AS STEVE CUT his way through the smooth black water of the port he was asking himself why he had run away from the woman. She was a remarkable woman, a terribly dangerous woman. Though no more beautiful than Lucinda Warburton or Rosalie, Mrs. Warburton was infinitely more disturbing. If he had remained five minutes longer in that cabin he was confident that he would have been bewitched by her.

From her came a subtle charm that was irresistible, given time to do its work. Her eyes were weirdly intriguing. Her figure was blatantly appealing—her appeal to a young healthy man was tremendous. And she had advertised in her first glance that he appealed to her. In self-defense he had been rude, had actually jeered at her and made friends with her assailant. And fearing intimacy during the row to the peninsula, he had left her in the man's hands and jumped overboard.

Of course she was in no further danger from Clews. The yachtsman was a gentleman who had assumed by the willingness of a married woman to board his yacht alone in the small hours of the morning that certain things were expected of him. When Mrs. Warburton screamed for help, he had been astounded. Steve chuckled. Come to think of it, there hadn't been one chance in a million that her cries would have been heard and a smaller chance that a rescuer would have appeared. Had Mrs. Warburton taken that into consideration when she screamed?

She did not impress him as a young woman who had many scruples. He thought she was about as unprincipled as one of the Greek goddesses whom she resembled. And he didn't want any part of her. She and Clews would have another bottle of champagne. Clews would apologize for his audacity and she would row ashore.

And all the time her elderly husband would be peacefully sleeping. Or would he? Would he be waiting a report from his trouble man?

It would be a very long time before Hutton would report the result of his visit to Stephen Cobb to his employer. Maybe they would meet in hell in a few years.

He touched bottom, waded ashore, skirted the town and reached his hut without encountering a soul. He needed a towel to dry himself, after which he would go back to the hummock and finish his night's sleep.

Pushing open the door, he entered, and immediately cut his foot on broken glass. He stopped short, stooped over and felt about gingerly with his hand. More broken glass.

Stepping backward to the door, he worked around by the wall to the stove and lighted a match.

His table was overturned and the kerosene lamp lay on the floor, its chimney shattered into bits. He discerned under a chair the flashlight which had fallen from the hand of the late Bertram Hutton. Securing this he turned it on and inspected the room. It was in great disorder. Tins of groceries had been broken open and misplaced. A suitcase which had stood against the wall lay on the floor open, its contents scattered about.

With an oath he picked up a chair, and avoiding the broken glass, set it under the rafter and climbed on it. As he had feared, the paper box containing the bonds was gone.

Three hours or more had passed since he had carried out the body of Hutton the trouble man. In his absence the place had been entered, ransacked, and the bonds stolen.

Steve went out of the house and sat on the step. For the first time since returning to Cobbport, he had something to worry him.

The loss of the bonds was bad enough, but their theft meant that Hutton had not been alone. Somebody had been lurking in the vicinity who had accomplished what Hutton had failed to do. This person knew that Hutton had been slain, and that the killer had packed the body on his back and carried it into the sea.

Apparently Steve had made a terrible mistake in not reporting the death of the burglar and standing on his rights as a householder. By getting rid of the body he had created the assumption of murder guilt.

Of course Warburton had the bonds. They were worth millions to him, and money was more important to him than the life of his trouble man. He would officially retire them as of six months back, and assume that Steve Cobb, lest he be accused of murder, would make no protest.

While the bonds were in Steve's possession, he could always go into court and get an injunction against the Cobb Company. But, the chance to block Warburton was gone.

So the thing to do was to get them back. It was four-thirty A.M. In an hour it would be daylight.

STEVE WENT BACK into the house and searched for the revolver which Hutton had owned and which had been laying on the floor when he had carried Hutton out. It was gone. The second house-breaker had found it, of course. He smiled wryly as it occurred to him that he could accuse neither of them of housebreaking.

They had just opened the door and walked in evidently unmolested.

Again detouring round the village he approached the Cobb estate along the shore. Posts had been set up at the boundary of the private beach, but the wires had not yet been strung. Glancing across the harbor he saw a mooring light on the yawl, but the portholes which had been lighted were now dark.

If Mrs. Warburton were not on the yawl still, he hoped she had reached home and had had time to fall asleep, because it was his intention to break into her husband's residence.

He left the beach and crossed the huge lawn which ran from the house down to the shore. As yet Warburton's gardeners had not had time to cut the grass which was long and contained sharp-edged weeds. After stepping on one of these weeds, Steve felt a twinge in the place on the sole of his left foot which the broken glass had cut. He had had too much on his mind to attend to that little cut.

The big house was in darkness. He had been afraid that Warburton was still up and around, since it could not have been more than an hour or two since he had received the bonds.

The servants slept on the third floor of the main house. The kitchen and pantry were located in an "L" at the rear, and he could force a window there with little chance of the slight sound disturbing the inmates of the residence.

The grounds were familiar to him from childhood, and he knew just which window to attack. Finding a sawhorse he stood on it, and using only a part of his great strength, he forced up the lower sash, despite the catch which fastened it. In a moment he stood in the great old-fashioned kitchen where he had begged cakes from the cook as a child.

The fact that he had neglected to bring with him Hutton's flashlight did not disturb him; he knew his way round this house in the dark. Of course he was not certain which was Warburton's room, but he assumed it was the huge corner room on the south end as its decorations were masculine, and it had been occupied in turn by his grandfather and father.

IN VIEW OF the nocturnal excursion of Mrs. Warburton, he doubted that she slept in the same room with her husband. If she happened to be with him, no matter. He could handle both of them.

He passed through the pantry and arrived in the front hall. At his left was the servants' stairway to the upper stories. The main stairway was opposite the front door and seventy or eighty feet from the pantry entrance.

Steve went softly up the servants' stairs. He went swiftly, as much at home in the dark as a bat or a mole. He stood at the top gazing speculatively down the long hall. Directly ahead the front stairs came up—there was a railing around them. The main corridor opened up at either side of the front stairs. There were nine rooms opening into it from the front of the house, six rooms on the rear side, all fine, big, solidly furnished, old-fashioned rooms, which were practically sound proof. The room probably occupied by Warburton was to the right at the end of the hall. Mrs. Warburton probably had the room on the front next her husband. Lucinda—well, it didn't matter where she slept. He hadn't come to call on Lucinda. She would have his mother's room which was very feminine in its furnishings and decorations and was opposite Ezra Cobb's room which ought to be occupied by Warburton.

He found the railing and saw dimly the corridor openings. He had no plan. He intended to trust to luck. It was unlikely that Warburton's door was locked. He would rush in, grasp the man in bed by the throat and force him to return the bonds or be choked to death.

As he laid his hand on the stair railing, there was a sound. A door had opened down the corridor. Suddenly the lights went on in the hall. Steve ducked back, but not before he had a glimpse of Warburton who had come out of the Ezra Cobb chamber. He was wearing a brilliant bathrobe and his head was bent. He walked twenty feet, opened the door of the room which Steve had assumed to be occupied by Mrs. Warburton, switched out the hall light and entered.

This was infuriating. If Mrs. Warburton had remained on the yawl her husband would raise the household when he found her room unoccupied. It might be full of guests for all Steve knew, and there were certainly six or eight servants.

If she had returned and was safely in bed there might be a confab lasting a long time. And, in less than an hour, it would be daylight. Should he retreat? Steve wasn't built that way.

Since he mustn't be found lurking in the hall in broad daylight, he would wait for his enemy in the man's room.

Softly he sped down the hallway, noiselessly turned the knob of Warburton's door, stepped inside and closed it behind him.

"What on earth do you want now?" asked a petulant and familiar female voice.

Mr. Stephen Cobb was so shocked and astounded that he stood at the door bereft of speech or motion. Click. A bed lamp went on.

"Dreams come true," exclaimed Mrs. Diana Warburton. "So you regretted lost opportunity."

She lay in the fine old four-poster bed, her black hair loose and falling in a lustrous mane upon her bare shoulders. Though her night dress was less revealing than her evening gown it was distracting. The sheet was pulled up only to her waist.

"I made a mistake," he muttered foolishly.

"Come here," she said sharply. "Come here or I shall scream."

Hesitatingly, he moved toward her. Though for three months he had gone about Cobbport naked save for swimming trunks, he was for the first time embarrassed by his nudeness.

"What do you mean by a mistake?" she demanded. "You are calling on me, are you not?"

"I—I thought this was his room," he faltered.

Her broad white brow knitted and her eyes snapped. "You were calling on my husband, then. Have you an appointment?"

Steve began to recover since it was apparent that she had no immediate intention of waking the house.

9

CAUGHT

"NOT EXACTLY," HE said grimly. "I want to see him more than he wants to see me."

"Hum. He has a gun, and he is a dead shot. I'm sure you will find it more agreeable here. Are you a burglar by any chance?"

"I'm after some property of mine which was stolen by his order tonight while I was—er—swimming."

She patted the bed beside her. "Sit here by me, Tarzan," she commanded. "Do as I say, do you hear?" Her voice rose shrilly.

Steve sat on the edge of the bed. A bitter-sweet disturbing perfume came from her person. Her great eyes had become luminous and she was smiling distractingly.

"You are a very handsome young man," she said softly. "And a rude young man. I ought to be very angry with you."

"Look here," he retorted. "You have a husband and the fellow on the yawl. How many men do you want?"

"I hate my husband, and Jack is only mildly entertaining. I have never encountered a man like you."

He jumped up. "I'm going. Good night."

"Sit down," she commanded. "I'll call my husband if you attempt to leave."

He smiled for the first time. "I dare you. If you do I'll tell him where you spent most of the night."

"I'm afraid you wouldn't. You go about like a savage, but you happen to be a gentleman. Sit down. I won't bite you."

Steve sat down sullenly. He was horribly embarrassed and somewhat alarmed. The woman was apparently lacking in modesty and eager to take advantage of an accident.

"Perhaps I can help you," she said softly. "What has my husband in his possession that you want? Aside from myself, of course."

He scowled at her angrily. "I don't want you, Mrs. Warburton," he declared.

Her eyes glittered. "You are going to want me very much," she replied. "You like me. I saw it in your eyes on the yawl. You ran away because you were afraid of me. Surely, Mr. Cobb, you haven't old-fashioned ideas about other men's wives."

"I don't like a woman who cheats on her husband," he said candidly.

Steve jumped up nervously. "I'm going," he said unsteadily. In three strides he was at the door.

"You come back here," she cried shrilly. If he had opened the door her cry would have alarmed the house. He had a mission and she mustn't be allowed to jeopardize it. Kid her along.

He returned to the bedside. "Mrs. Warburton," he said, "you are a very beautiful woman, and I have good reason not to like your husband. But I'm a bit romantic. For example, I like to do the love-making. I resent being taken captive, so to speak."

She smiled dazzlingly. "And you're quite right. But

this was such a golden opportunity. Sit down again, my dear boy. Let's begin to get acquainted." Reluctantly and gingerly he seated himself on the edge of the bed.

"Suppose we meet tomorrow in town—" he began and his voice froze in his throat.

For the door was thrown open and Warburton stood in the doorframe. He had a leveled automatic in his right hand.

"Caught you, eh?" he snarled. "What—by Heaven!"

"If you had only waited a few minutes," said the lady in the bed mockingly.

"My wife's lover, eh?" he said. His eyes narrowed.

He lifted his weapon. "William, don't be a fool," screamed Mrs. Warburton. "You'll have to stand trial."

Steve was on his feet, his hands swinging loosely at his side. He could read the man's mind as if it were an open book. He had the bonds, but he needed Steve Cobb out of the way. And he had entered his wife's room and found Cobb, almost nude, on the bed with Mrs. Warburton. With his money, he could get himself acquitted on the Unwritten Law. He proposed to kill Steve Cobb. But he must not kill his wife.

"I'm not your wife's lover," he said loudly. "I thought this was your room. I came to see you, Warburton."

"You lie," ejaculated Warburton, stepping into the room. "I know her. She told me tonight she wanted you."

"And I didn't come alone," shouted Steve. "Grab him, Jack."

IT WAS A desperate device, but it worked. Warburton half turned and Steve was already flying through the air.

Warburton fired as he fell, but the bullet went through

the ceiling. The young giant was on top of him. His knee pinioned his enemy's right wrist, and he tore the weapon loose with his left hand.

Doors were slamming. There were screams and shouts in the house. Steve shifted the barrel to his hand and struck Warburton on top of the head with the metal hilt. He leaped to his feet, rushed to the window, shoved out the screen and leaped upon the roof of the porch. As he glanced back, he saw Lucinda Warburton in her night gown rush into the room and fall on her knees beside the body of her father. And he saw the amazing Mrs. Warburton waving to him a cheerful adieu.

"Father, father," wailed Lucinda.

"He'll be all right," Mrs. Warburton assured her. "Get some water and throw it in his face."

The girl rushed into the bathroom and Warburton stirred and sat up, holding his head. Servants were assembling at the door.

"What was it, Mr. Warburton, sir?" demanded the butler. "Robbers?"

"Yes, robbers," said the millionaire harshly.

"Shall I call the police?"

"It won't do any good. Clear out, all of you."

Lucinda came forth with a pitcher of water. "Oh, you're all right," she cried happily. "Was it a robber, father?"

"Yes," he said curtly.

From the bed came an ironical laugh.

Warburton got heavily on his feet and moved toward his wife.

"You she devil," he growled. "He came here to rob me. Damn him!"

"Of what you hold dearest, your wife," she said insolently.

Making an inarticulate noise, the wretched husband strode from the room. Lucinda lingered.

"What do you mean?" she demanded of her step-mother.

"Your father came in at an unfortunate moment," the woman said brazenly.

Lucinda stepped nearer. "I saw him. It was Steve Cobb," she said tensely.

"A darling boy," remarked the woman in the bed.

"I don't believe that he's your lover," the girl exclaimed hotly. "He wouldn't—he's not like that."

Mrs. Warburton's eyes narrowed. "Your father found us together and he was going to shoot Steve, so he must have thought so."

The girl's eyes filled with tears. "You are wicked—wicked! My father ought to divorce you—"

"It would be so nice if he would," replied her step-mother. "Good night, Lucinda, darling."

STEVE REACHED THE beach before he slowed up. He should not have left without the bonds. But, if he had remained he would have been overpowered by the servants. He had lost his chance. And Warburton would get them into a safe place immediately. Send them to his bank vault.

The man had intended to murder him. It was visible in his eyes. And from now on his life would not be safe. Warburton had to get him out of the way.

He plunged into the sea, swam about for a few minutes, and emerged feeling much better. As he strode along the shore toward the village in the gray dawn he noticed that the green yawl had disappeared.

At nine in the morning, Silas Cobb, who was a cousin ten times removed, of Steve Cobb, found the young man outside the post office when he came to open up.

"Mornin', Steve."

"Mornin', Silas."

"Should think you'd be fishin' this morning."

"Feel lazy."

Silas unlocked the door and went inside the tiny post office. Steve followed him in and was at his heels when he went back of the partition.

"Expecting a letter?" inquired Silas.

"Yep."

Steve leaned back on a wooden chair and Silas seated himself on his cushioned high stool behind the little window through which he transacted business. As was his custom, he deftly removed from its wrapper a copy of last night's Boston *Transcript*, and began to peruse the news of the world. Steve twiddled his thumbs. He was wearing a sweater over his bathing trunks today, and white sneakers, because he had a cut on one of his feet.

Various people came in to buy stamps or to post letters. It came to be ten o'clock and a voice came through the wicket which caused Steve to grow tense.

"Good morning, Mr. Warburton," said the postmaster.

"I said good morning. Send this registered mail and give me a receipt for it."

There was pushed through the window a thick Manila envelope. Silas stamped it, put more seals on it, tossed it in his wire basket and busied himself with the receipt. Warburton pushed a packet of stamped letters through

the window, took his receipt and departed. He had not
seen Steve Cobb.

Other people came to the window and the basket filled
up.

"Hi, Steve, dump these in the mail bag," requested the
postmaster. "Slocom will drive up for the mail any minute
now."

Steve picked up the wire basket and emptied its contents
into the open maw of the mail bag, but not the registered
envelope which he slipped under his sweater.

"I'll be moseying along, Silas," he remarked.

"How about your letter?"

"Pick it up later. Want to get out in the Bay."

The young man was grinning broadly as he hastened to
his little house. He had calculated just what Warburton
would do.

AFTER THE VISITATION of the night before he would send
the bonds to New York at top speed. Instead of entrusting
the mail to a servant he had brought it personally to the
post office. And, inside the partition, Steve Cobb had been
lurking and he had got back his own.

Shutting the door, he sat down to inspect the registered letter. Hours ago he had cleaned up the mess in his
residence and repaired the damage done by Warburton's
emissary as much as possible.

He looked at the address and lifted his eyebrows. The
bonds were being sent to Henry Pennypacker, Cedar
Street, New York, and marked personal.

So Pennypacker had sold out. Pennypacker had been
his father's lawyer and was deep in the plot to defraud the
son. Well, he had never much liked Henry Pennypacker.

"Wonder what the penalty is," he said aloud as he stared whimsically at the globs of sealing wax. Like most people who live alone he talked to himself quite a little. "Well, I don't think Warburton would care to describe contents."

He broke each seal slowly, deliberately and with keen enjoyment. It was something to have outguessed old Warburton.

He drew out the contents, smiling broadly and his smile faded out and was replaced by consternation. There were no bonds in the envelope. There were three copies of a contract occupying four pages of foolscap. And there was a personal letter.

"In for a penny, in for a pound," he said softly, and began to whistle under his breath as he opened the letter.

"Dear Henry," he read, "As a certain party refuses to do business, being actuated no doubt by malice, and, as I cannot make a move while he maintains this attitude, you need trouble yourself no further. I shall handle the situation in my own way. W. Warburton."

Steve folded the letter, replaced it with the contracts in the torn envelope and gazed ruefully at the envelope.

"Robbed the mails," he muttered. "May get Silas into terrible trouble. Well, maybe I can fix that."

10

THE CENTENARIAN

"HELLO, STEVE," SAID a high pitched slightly cracked voice. "What you doin' there?"

With a guilty gesture Steve covered up the contents of the stolen envelope. He grinned sheepishly at the individual who had darkened his door.

"Hello, General," he said, "Come on in."

There entered a queer, bowed, wrinkled ancient who leaned heavily on a hickory cane. There was no hair whatever on the head of this creature and his face was a network of deep lines. His brows hung over his eyes but could not conceal their brightness. They shone like lamps in the dim light of the hut. He smiled, revealing two rows of perfect teeth, so perfect that their falseness was obvious. He caught the end of his long pendulous nose between thumb and forefinger and pulled on it satirically and hobbled to the sofa where he sat down heavily and wagged his head at the youth.

"You looked worried, Steve," he piped up. "Quit it. Ain't nothing worth worrying about. Ax me, I know."

Steve gazed at him fondly. This was General Seth Burton who was enjoying his hundred and first year. This pack of bones on the sofa had been a drummer boy in the

Mexican War of 1846 and a General of Division in the Civil War. He had lived so long he hadn't a relative left in the world. He had made a great fortune in the seventies and lost it in the nineties. He existed comfortably upon a Federal pension. He was neither senile nor helpless. He was a philosopher and Steve Cobb was his pupil.

"I was going to drop in and have a talk with you this afternoon, General," declared Steve.

"I seen you come out of the post office, boy. You had something on your mind. You walked too fast. You acted like you wasn't happy."

"Nonsense. I'm fine, General."

"Kind of bothers you to have people living in the Cobb Mansion, eh?" demanded the old fellow.

"No, no. Not at all."

The old man pounded on the floor with his cane.

"What's the use of anything?" he demanded. "Nothing. Ain't I told you that it's going 'gainst nature to bother. Here I thought I had you all converted and you got notions. I'm disappointed in you Steve."

Steve laughed. At the moment his troubles seemed trifles for such was the effect of the centenarian upon his pupil.

"Everything's all right," he said with his customary cheerful grin.

"Seen you on the beach talking to that Warburton young woman," stated the old man. "Mighty purty. What you want to do is think how she's goin' to look fifty years from now. They ain't worth a man's time, lad."

"I don't give a hoot about her," declared Steve earnestly.

"I seen you," said the General mournfully. "There was

a girl I was in love with in 1855 or was it 56—I disremember. Lost my silly head about her. She threw me over. Heh! Heh! She died in 1874. That was sixty years ago. I was going to commit suicide in 1856 about her. Heh, heh! What a fool I'd have been."

"I'm not in love with this girl, I told you."

"My old friend Daniel Sickles," continued the visitor. "He loved that girl that threw me down. What did he do? He married her. Caught her with another man. He fought a duel about her. Heh! Heh! Might have been killed. Worthless woman. All women are worthless. Bear that in mind, boy. Say, I remember Dan at Gettysburg. I bring him an order to withdraw his division to the main Federal line. Meade sent me up. He was a General, then, Dan was. He had only one leg but he was a fighter. Dan sez to me with that grin of his, 'Seth, you go back and tell that whiskered old grampus to bring the Army up to my position. Here I am and here I stay till hell freezes over.'

"And do you know what Meade did? By God, he brung the whole army up to where Dan Sickles was fighting the Rebs. That's how we won the battle."

"You and your old crony Sickles both should have been court-marshaled," said Steve, grinning with delight.

The General cackled gleefully. "Sure we should but Meade didn't have the guts to do it."

He rambled on and Steve listened.

"Live only for the eternal—the wind, the waves, the hills, the trees and the earth, boy. Everything else passes away. Your passions pass and your anger. Forget people; eat, sleep, work just enough to get food and lodgings. That's the only way to be happy." He shook his head. "I thought I had you converted."

"GENERAL," SAID STEVE earnestly, "It's all right for you but I'm young. I thought I was converted. I've never been so happy as since I met you and settled down here, but there was a man I hated and I knew the way to punish him. All I had to do was to wait, bide my time. The longer I waited, the worse his punishment would be. That's why I was willing to lay flat on my back and drink in the sun and the air. I had a stick to hit him with when the time came and now I've lost my stick."

"You're a fool. He'll be dead in ten years, or twenty or thirty. Maybe sooner if he don't take care of himself and eat simple food like I do. He'll cut his own stick to hit himself with."

Steve laughed. "If I could depend on that."

"You can." The old man rose, moved toward Steve and inspected him shrewdly from close range with his small bright black eyes.

"Late last night I was on the beach, Steve," he said in a low tone. "I don't need much sleep, you know. I was sitting there contemplating the infinite I was. And then you came. What was it you was carrying, Steve?"

"Eh? Nothing," gasped Steve, who turned pale.

"Looked to me like a man you was carrying, Steve. I hope you ain't done nothing you hadn't ought to do."

"My conscience is clean," declared the young man whose lips were very dry.

"Yeh? I seen you come ashore, too. You wasn't carrying nothing on your back. You was hours in the sea? What were you doing in the sea, Steve?"

"Swimming," said Steve.

General Burton laid his hand on the youth's shoulder and squeezed it with surprising strength. "I've killed men in my day—in battle, in private warfare. I was a hard, brutal man in my day, and I'm sorry for it. I don't hold with courts and judges any more. I let nature take her course. If your conscience is clean, I think, perhaps, I was asleep on the beach last night, Steve. And I dreamed."

Steve caught the wrinkled gnarled hand and squeezed it in both of his. "God bless you, general," he said brokenly. "You're my only friend, I guess."

"Well, I got to be going down to the post office to see if there's a letter for me. 'Side from the pension letter every month nobody has wrote me for twenty years. Cause why? Cause everybody that would write me has been dead that long. Don't be a fool, now, Steve. Glad you lost this stick you mentioned. 'Vengeance is mine, saith the Lord.'"

For some time after the centenarian had departed, Steve sat there silent and absorbed in bitter reflections. He was a murderer and a mail robber. He could cover the mail robbery by posting the contents of the registered letter to Pennypacker in an ordinary envelope. The contracts undoubtedly would be delivered and the lawyer would have no reason to inquire of Warburton whether he hadn't been careless in not registering them.

There were at least two witnesses to the murder, however; the General, who would keep his mouth shut, being friendly and, despite his age, in full possession of his faculties, and the unknown who had stolen the bonds.

He had to get the bonds back. Without them, he couldn't

settle down to the humdrum happy existence the General preached. And how to get them?

Warburton would see to it that another attempt to enter the big house would be blocked and Warburton wasn't in the least likely to keep them there any length of time. Evidently he didn't trust them to the mails. He would send them to New York by special messenger.

He secured an envelope from a table drawer, addressed it to Pennypacker and sealed up in it the contents of the registered envelope. After that he carefully burned the registered envelope. Having destroyed evidence of the post office robbery he rose, envelope in his hand and stepped outside to utter an exclamation of astonishment and apprehension.

Warburton was coming up the path and was only twenty feet distant.

The millionaire was wearing riding clothes and a groom was standing below holding two horses.

He bowed coldly to Stephen Cobb.

"May I have a few minutes of your time?" he asked politely.

Steve gazed at him insolently.

"I've nothing to say to you, sir," he replied.

11

"WHO STOLE THE BONDS?"

"YOU WILL FIND it to your advantage to give me an interview in view of the circumstances of our last meeting," retorted Warburton.

"Thinks he can buy me off now that he has the bonds," said Steve to himself. "Don't suppose he would have them on him."

He stepped aside and Warburton entered the hut, gazing about him contemptuously.

"Do you mean to say that you live in this hovel?" he demanded.

"More contentedly than you do in your mansion, Mr. Warburton," said Steve who had followed him inside.

"I sent an agent to see you last night," said Warburton. "A man named Frank Hutton—"

"Oh, your trouble man."

"You've heard of him, eh? Well, he has not returned. What became of him?"

Steve shrugged his shoulders.

"How should I know?"

"Didn't he call on you?"

"I was out most of the night."

"Hump. He hasn't returned."

"Seems to me that's your loss, Mr. Warburton."

Warburton tapped his right riding boot with his crop. "I'm not going to bandy words with you," he said loudly. "I am considering having you arrested for attempted robbery."

"Well?"

"If you are arrested you will be convicted, young man."

Steve grinned.

"Will Mrs. Warburton be a witness against me?"

Warburton grinned sourly. "She will," he declared. "If she refused, she would be giving me grounds for divorce. My wife, young man, is a woman with a highly developed sense of humor. She has no desire to be divorced, however, and she will testify that you broke into our house and were robbing her chamber when I interrupted you."

"So what?" demanded Steve.

"So you had better listen to reason. I will overlook the events of last night on condition that you sell me those bonds. I'll pay a hundred thousands dollars."

Steve stared at him.

"Why do you think I broke into your house?" he asked slowly.

"Because my wife, who is young and impulsive, was indiscreet enough to say something to you which made you suppose she would not object to your clandestine visit."

"Do you really think that?" muttered Steve Cobb.

"Damn it, what else can I think?" shouted Warburton, whose temper could no longer be restrained.

"You wrong your wife," said Steve gravely. "I went there for another purpose. I went after something which belongs to me which I wanted."

The millionaire glared at him and suddenly his face

lightened. "Do you mean that the bonds are hidden in my house?" he cried excitedly.

Steve's hands clenched. This was not pretense. Warburton didn't have the bonds and didn't know where they were. Steve saw in his face the intention of tearing the house apart, pulling it down if necessary. The bonds were worth fifty times the value of the old house to him. And Steve loved the house. He didn't want it pulled down.

"I'm not fool enough for that," he replied; "The bonds are in a safe place. There is an heirloom—something of my grandfather's. I wanted it."

"You young idiot, I will give it to you gladly. Come. Let's do business."

"I'll do no business with you. My father did—to his sorrow."

"Then, by God, I'll have you arrested as a burglar."

"Shoot," said Steve Cobb. "This is my house. Get out of it."

His face in flame, Warburton lifted his riding crop. Steve measured him derisively.

"Don't," he said. "You're an old man. I'd probably tear you apart."

"You'll hear from me," cried his enemy. "Damn you, I'll force you to disgorge."

"Please convey my respects to Mrs. Warburton."

With a growl of rage the millionaire rushed out of the hut. Steve sat limply down upon the couch.

If Warburton didn't have the bonds, who had stolen them? Nobody save Warburton, Pennypacker and himself were aware of their existence. Stay, one other. Hutton, who was dead and out in the Atlantic, his body bobbing up and down upon the boundless ocean.

Who had visited his hut, torn the place apart, taken the bonds and fled?

IN THIS QUIET hamlet there was a bold cunning thief, probably a witness to the murder of Hutton and who expected to prevent action by Steve Cobb by threatening to accuse him of the killing.

To the devil with the communion with wind, wave and earth preached by General Seth Burton. He'd find the thief and get back his property if he had to commit another killing.

Steve rose and strode out of the hut and went swiftly to the post office where he posted his letter.

The postmaster, not being busy, scrutinized the address.

"That's funny," he said, "Mr. Warburton sent a registered letter to this same feller this morning. It was when you was here."

Steve grinned. "Nothing funny about that. Pennypacker was one of my father's lawyers and he is now working for Warburton."

"Well," said Seth. "It's what you might call one of them coincidences."

Steve nodded. "Have there been any strangers in town yesterday and today that you noticed?"

The postmaster shook his head.

"Nobody but automobile tourists that went straight through. None that I've seen."

Steve strolled dolefully down to the shore. The sun danced upon the waters of the bay and the gentle waves broke into creamy lather as they rolled upon the strand but they didn't tempt him today. Up on the beach he could see Warburton's workmen building the barrier and depriving the natives of what they considered their privilege to use the bathing beach.

Coming down the beach was a very trim young woman in a bathing suit with a Chinese coolie coat covering her to the hips. Even at that distance he was aware that she had exceptional legs.

Lucinda. Lucinda had come into her step-mother's room as Steve departed from it, but she might not have recognized him and it wasn't likely that Mrs. Warburton or her irate husband would offer her explanations. However, he didn't want to see Lucinda. The thing to do was to scram. But Steve didn't move. His depression was so profound he could think only of his loss.

A stick, he had told the General. Rather it was a sixteen-inch gun with which to blow the despoiler of his father into smithereens when the time came.

He had expected that he would have to wait a year or two. Depression times were not suitable to huge stock issues and Warburton would be able to renew his notes for the vast sums he had borrowed to push over the Cobb company only so long. He had to put out millions of securities to cover his borrowings and that was when Steve intended to come in.

So it had been like a vacation for Steve, this waiting period. No wonder he had relaxed and embraced the philosophy of the old General—with reservations.

Lucinda was approaching. She was abreast of him. She passed. So he was either a burglar or a libertine in her opinion. Suddenly she turned and bore down on him. She put her little hands upon her hips and stared at him gravely. To his annoyance, Steve felt the blood rushing to his face.

Steve picked up a handful of sand and let it dribble through his fingers watching the operation as though absorbed.

"Beast," said Lucinda venomously.

"Move right along," requested Steve.

"Rotter," she said shrilly.

"You really have very good legs," remarked the rotter.

LUCINDA SQUATTED SUDDENLY and made a pitiful effort to conceal her legs with her short Coolie coat.

"It's a pity my father didn't shoot you," she cried furiously.

"The thing for a young lady to do when she encounters a beast and a rotter," Steve stated coldly, "is to pass right along hurriedly, holding her skirt, provided she has one, to avoid contamination."

"A woman old enough to be your mother," she said contemptuously. "A wicked, nasty woman."

Steve wagged his head. "That's no way to speak about your beautiful young step-mother," he said reproachfully.

"I knew that you were a stupid brute," said the girl remorselessly, "but I didn't think you were a lascivious one. I'd sooner think that you were a burglar than that."

"As a matter of fact, I am a burglar," said Steve. "I am one of the most skillful burglars in America. I came down here on a vacation after robbing a lot of banks and I was just trying to keep my hand in.

"I also am a gangster and in my odd moments I go around burning down churches."

"That's what you look like," said Lucinda, "but Mrs. Warburton says you are her lover."

"She was kidding," he assured her more earnestly that he supposed. "Your father is going to have me arrested for burglary. He told me so this morning.

"But you know he daren't, on account of her," she said passionately. "I just want to tell you that I have a gun and know how to use it—"

"I wouldn't think of breaking into your room—" he said hastily. Her cheeks flamed.

"Why, you—I mean if you go near my step-mother again, I'll shoot you without the slightest hesitation."

"Okay. Shoot straight. I'd hate to be crippled or maimed."

To his consternation the girl threw herself flat on the beach and sobbed loudly.

"Listen, kid," Steve cried remorsefully, "I'm sorry. Darn it, don't cry. It was just an accident that I got into your mother's room—"

"That woman isn't my mother—"

"I beg your pardon. Mrs. Warburton's room. Honestly, I didn't have any understanding with her. I only saw her once before in my life. I went in there to get something I wanted. Something that belongs to me—I mean it's something that used to belong to me."

Lucinda's big eyes studied him. Her lower lip ceased to quiver.

"Really? Truly?"

"That's a fact."

"But you broke into the house. We found a kitchen window forced. You are a thief."

"Oh, sure. Why not? What's a little stealing?"

"I happen to know that you are a well bred man though you don't give much indication of it. So you would lie anyway. It's not necessary. She boasted to me that you and she are lovers."

Steve shrugged his shoulders. "Where are we getting by this interview?" he demanded.

"I'm sure my father would be glad to give you any object which you particularly cherished in the old house. He was kindly disposed toward you until last night. Just what did you want?"

"An antimacassar," he stammered. It was the first word which came into his mind which was the more curious since he hadn't the least notion just what was an antimacassar.

"There is none in that room," she said in a hard tone.

"Well, I thought it was in that room."

"What is an antimacassar?" she demanded scornfully. "Why you don't even know."

"That's my story," he said sullenly.

"When I think that you soiled my lips," she cried passionately. "Oh, I could kill you, you hulking behemoth!"

Steve began to get angry at last. "Listen," he said harshly. "All I've had from you has been abuse from our first meeting. You persist in seeking me out and calling me names. Do you know what I think of you?"

"I don't want to know!"

"Men have spoiled you because your father is rich. You think because I kissed you that day that I was infatuated with you. You've got an exaggerated notion of your importance and your looks and what you can get away with. You gave me a pain that day and every time I've seen you since.

I wouldn't like you, if your father wasn't a brigand and a pirate—"

She leaped to her feet. "Don't you dare abuse my father," she cried. "Just because he was a smarter man than your father and because you're broke and too worthless to go to work and lay around on beaches and make love to vicious middle-aged women, you're vindictive and mean-spirited and you insult me because I'm a girl and can't hit back. I'll show you if I'm helpless. I've influence with my father. He ought to have divorced that woman long ago. I'll make him divorce her and name you as correspondent or else I'll have you put in jail as a common burglar. You see if I don't."

Hurling at him a glare of hate she ran at top speed back toward the Cobb estate.

Steve scowled after her and then smiled. "Well," he drawled, "I suppose I brought it on myself. Anyway she's Warburton's kid and therefore poisonous. Confound her, she's so damn pretty that I might make a fool of myself if I didn't keep her off. It's a cinch she'll never speak to me again. That's swell."

He rose and returned slowly to the village. He was a Cape Cod beachcomber and no mistake if he couldn't recover the bonds. No income whatever. And it was one thing to live like a hermit and make the sea feed him when he knew the life wouldn't last more than a year or two, but quite another to be forced to scratch a living this way indefinitely.

Poor little Lucinda who had a crook for a father and a wanton for a stepmother. No wonder she was always belligerent. No wonder she was full of venom. Give her a break and she might be a nice kid.

12

THE VILLAGE SLEUTH

HE CAST A backward glance along the shore and observed that the green yawl was beating into the harbor. He grinned as he wondered if the remarkable Mrs. Warburton had made a date with its owner for tonight.

As he was passing the post office, Eben Cobb, a remote relative, came out of the Souvenir store opposite which he owned and beckoned. "Hey, Steve. Want to see you a minute."

Eben was a typical Cape character, a man of sixty who wore policeman's suspenders over his shirt and was always coatless. Upon the right suspender was pinned a carefully shined silver badge which read Cobbport Chief of Police. Eben was not only Chief but the police force as well. As the job paid a pittance, he earned a living running a souvenir and notion shop in a village which was off the state road and therefore not much frequented by tourists. Incidentally his souvenirs were badly chosen and slow moving.

"Got to ax you questions," he stated importantly. "Police business."

Steve grinned. "Fire away," he invited.

"Wall, it seems that a man named Frank Hutton, whose

He whipped a revolver from his pocket.

a guest of Mr. Warburton's, left there last night and ain't been seen hair or hide of."

"You don't say?"

"Yes siree," said the Chief emphatically. "And Mr. Warburton was in here personally and talked to me. He suspects foul play, he does."

"I'm shocked," said Steve gravely.

"Seems he set out to call on you," said the Chief, pulling reflectively at his gray goatee and gazing sharply at Steve with his small pale blue eyes.

"Not likely. Don't know him."

"He comes down here 'bout eleven o'clock and he asks the gas station boy where you lived."

"Sort of late for calling, eh?"

Eben nodded. "That's what I ben thinkin'. Howsomever, he had your house pinted out to him, and he was seen going up that way. And nobody has seen him since, Steve." This was said most dramatically.

"Eleven o'clock," remarked Steve. "Well, now, Eben, I can't help you. I didn't sleep in the house last night. I went up on the hummock with a blanket like I often do. You know that."

"Yep. You know it's my duty to investigate."

"Sure. And how you love it," Steve said with a grin.

"Now about this robbery at your house."

"Robbery?"

Eben cackled. He was a wisp of a man swelled with his own importance.

"Ain't nothing gets by me. I seen Myra Sears." He cocked his head to one side like a cheeky sparrow. "Myra says she seen a light in your place and she went up and woke you up and told you there were robbers. You went down there—"

"And there was nobody there," said Steve tartly.

"That's what you told her—but Myra says she heard a racket and voices."

"Myra was using her imagination. She came to the house and saw there was nobody in it."

"That's your story."

"Eben," said Steve sternly. "I'm going to grab your whiskers and pull them out by the roots if you insinuate—"

"I ain't insinuating," Eben declared hastily. "But it's very suspicious, it seems to me."

"You seem to insinuate that a guest of Mr. Warburton's went down and broke into my house. Isn't that absurd?"

"I ain't sayin' it was this Mr. Hutton. Don't seem likely—"

"YOU'RE INVESTIGATING THE disappearance of Hutton. Whether or not there was a burglary at my house is no affair of yours unless I lodge a charge."

"Maybe it wasn't burglary. Maybe Mr. Hutton that was

inquiring for you went up to your place and you and him had a ruction—"

Steve grasped the gray goatee and twisted it until the chief of police howled.

"It's not likely that a guest of Mr. Warburton would call on a man he didn't know at eleven o'clock at night," the young man declared. "Forget it."

"Wall," said Eben doggedly. "I ben up to your place, and you not being to home, I looked round. I seen evidence of things being broken. I seen glass, lots of broken glass in your ash barrel. And this is what I dug out of the door jamb with my penknife."

He held up between thumb and forefinger a leaden bullet.

Steve gasped but instantly rallied. "You chump," he said, laughing, "that's probably been there for ages. I never noticed it myself. I give you credit for being a smart investigator, though, Eben. Not one policeman in a thousand would have dug out that bullet."

"I ain't no fool," said Eben complacently. "I keep up to date by reading detective stories."

"Now let me tell you something," declared Steve. "See that green yawl? She was here last night but gone this morning when I woke up. That ought to suggest something to a bright mind like yours."

"What?" demanded Eben.

"Not finding me at home, if he ever did call on me, Hutton might have gone out to the yawl. No doubt its owner is a friend of Warburton's. And the yawl might have taken him down to Woods Hole where he could get a train for somewhere."

"By gosh," exclaimed Eben. "I bet that's what happened. I'll go out and have a talk with the folks on that boat."

Steve, however, was considerably perturbed as he went on to his house. There had been plenty of breakage which he had swept up and deposited in the ash barrel. The bullet was one of those fired by Hutton, of course. He had a clear case of self defense in the killing of Hutton, and he had destroyed it by concealing the killing and getting rid of the body. The frightful part of it all was that his defense of his bonds had been to no purpose. They were gone. And if a thick-headed local constable like Eben could discover as much as he had turned up, what might a competent police detective find.

"I'm a double-distilled fool," Steve said dismally as he pushed open his door and entered his tiny house.

THE OFFICES OF William Warburton and Company occupied half a floor of a high building on Broadway near Wall Street. At ten on the morning following the events of the last chapter, Mr. Warburton entered his private office and there filed in after him his three partners, if men who received a very small percentage of the annual profits of the concern could be called his partners.

"Have an easy trip from the Cape, sir?" asked Partner James Worth solicitously.

"Tedious, but swift and satisfactory. I left the Cape landing field at seven and here I am. What's the Washington report, Worth?"

Mr. Worth, who was a spruce young man with a brown mustache, smiled complacently. "Splendid, sir. I've had an interview with the attorney general in person, discussed the new Securities Act and he agrees with me that there is no longer the slightest reason for holding up legitimate stock issues since the perilous clauses in the former Securities Act have been eliminated."

"Oh," said Warburton thoughtfully. "Mr. Brown."

"Prospectuses on the Cobb Concrete Company are prepared, sir, and I have gone over them. They are quite satisfactory. There is every reason for an increase of capitalization from ten to twenty-five million dollars and our banks are ready to underwrite the issue. With the vast boom in building industries due to the Federal expenditure of billions, all development work, plants, imports and such are perfectly justifiable and sure to be very profitable. The N.R.A. is much pleased with our intention to double our working forces at a ten per cent increase in wages. I had a talk with the President of the Mammouth Bank who holds a good many of our notes and he was very much pleased."

"Nevertheless," said Warburton, "we've got to hold things up. We're not ready."

"But why not?" demanded Mr. Brown. "I have everything ready. The underwriting is arranged as I have explained. It's a matter of engraving the stock certificates—that's all."

"Hold things up. I didn't expect the Washington end would be cleared up so soon—" To himself he added: "I hoped it wouldn't."

Brown looked very grave. "We can't hold things up," he persisted. "We're extended like the devil. The Cobb Company is the only thing we have which we can put over in a big way at this time. We have three millions in loans coming due in four weeks. I've had no intimation from the banks that they will be called, but if we don't float the Cobb

Issues, they are apt to think there is something wrong and call our loans pronto."

Warburton bit his lip. "I expect to be ready in a week or ten days," he said. "Something has come up that I want to look into—"

"Nothing I hope which affects the Cobb Issues," said the third partner, Mr. Price, anxiously. "It's our ace, Mr. Warburton."

"Nothing serious. Go back to your desks, gentlemen. That's all."

After they had gone, the president of the company sat at his desk staring into vacancy. His business was "Other People's Business." His firm created nothing, but hung about like a vulture to swoop upon an industry which was in difficulties and which promised juicy pickings. The Cobb company had been a prize—nothing wrong with it except depression and need of immediate cash. It had taken all that Warburton possessed and had been able to borrow to push the Cobb Company into the precipice, but its tangible assets were great and after he had floated the new securities he could pay off his loans and retain control of the concern without an actual cent of cash invested.

His was a magnificent office. Outside a score of clerks and typists worked steadily. The bright young men who were his partners knew nothing of the seamy side of the firm. That was all under Warburton's hat. It looked like a powerful legitimate business enterprise, that of Warburton's, but the head of the firm took what he wanted any way he could get it and he had employees too disreputable to show their noses on lower Broadway.

EVERYTHING CONNECTED WITH the Cobb Corporation

had seemed set. As far as the loans were concerned, the banks, knowing the situation, would not press Warburton for them until Congress had made it possible to carry on refinancing without peril to the financers. But if the Cobb Issues did not come out at the first opportunity, they'd jump the firm of Warburton and Company.

Warburton had been in possession of the Cobb Company for a month before the horrid discovery was made of the existence of a forgotten bond issue which throttled expansion. Under existing laws, ignorance was no excuse for misrepresentation. If Warburton refinanced without having secured and retired the bonds, he could be sent to jail.

There had been another six weeks in an effort to locate Steve Cobb who owned the bonds, whom Warburton had assumed to be laying low thirsting for revenge and waiting for his opportunity. There was the bright light of hope when it was found that Steve was loafing at Cobbport and that the bonds, apparently, were in his possession there.

And then Hutton, who rarely failed, had failed and disappeared. And Cobb laughed at offers to purchase his securities and impudently inaugurated an affair with the wife of the new owner of the Cobb Company.

Warburton, sitting down to dinner on the Cape, had been informed by phone that Washington had given its "O.K." and all that was necessary was his consent to the flotation of the big stock issue. It had brought him post haste to New York to hold up the business until he knew where he stood.

Unused to being thwarted, Warburton fumed as he sat at his desk. He refused to answer telephone calls and scowled at his secretaries who dared to open his door. Finally the door opened and a heavy footed, heavy jowled man with a derby hat and big hands walked into the Presence.

"Detective Sergeant Murphy from Police Headquarters," he announced.

"How in hell did you get in here and what in hell do you want?" roared the capitalist.

"I forced my way in, if you want to know," said the cop truculently. "I been waiting out there for fifteen minutes and them rabbits you have working for you was afraid to tell you I had to see you."

Warburton forced a smile. "Sorry," he said in a different tone. "I was busy and didn't want to be interrupted, but I am always at the service of the authorities."

"That's fine," grinned Sergeant Murphy. "You got a man in this office named Frank Hutton?"

"Not exactly. That is the name of one of my field men."

"Where is he now, Mr. Warburton?"

"I would like to find out," said the millionaire eagerly. "I haven't heard from him for several days."

The policeman took a big envelope from his pocket, opened it and drew forth a salt water stained wallet with the initials F.H. on it, and a mass of soggy papers.

"Some of these are visiting cards with his name and this address on them," the officer stated. "They deciphered that somehow down at headquarters."

Warburton turned slowly pale.

"What does this mean?" he asked anxiously.

"The Coast Guard boat, Tecumseh, picked up a corpse in Nantucket Sound yesterday. He was clothed, boots and all, and no water in his stomach so he must have been killed.

Big bruise on his forehead. Murdered and thrown overboard from somewhere."

"Good God!"

"Hadn't been in the water more than twenty-four hours by the looks of him. Think you could identify him?"

Warburton shuddered. "I—I don't know."

"When and where did you last see him?"

"WHY—WHY, HE WAS at my house at Cobbport on Cape Cod. He—er—left the house—this is Friday—it was Tuesday evening for—er—a walk. He didn't return. I notified the local chief of police that he had disappeared and asked him to make inquiries, the next day."

"Cobbport. Is that on the south side of Cape Cod?"

"Yes. On the Nantucket Sound."

"It's him all right," said Murphy with satisfaction. "Sure. They found the body off Nantucket. Think of that now!"

"It's most distressing!" said Warburton from the heart.

"It lets us out," said Murphy with satisfaction. "The feller was murdered all right, but in Massachusetts. You come with me and identify him and then we hand Massachusetts a nice murder mystery and good luck to them."

"I—I'll send a man who knows Hutton with you, Sergeant. It would be too painful to me."

"Why? You and him have a quarrel?" demanded the policeman sharply.

"No, no. Not at all. I don't want to look at a partly decomposed corpse."

Murphy's suspicion vanished. "I don't think nothing of it," he declared. "But a lot of folks are like that. How about his wife and family?"

"I believe he was a bachelor."

"Well, his landlady, then. We need a couple of identi-
fications."

Warburton pressed a buzzer. A young woman entered.

"Get me the address of Frank P. Hutton, please,"
requested the head of the firm.

In a moment she returned with an address typed on a
slip of paper which she gave to her employer and which
he handed to the officer.

"Murray Hill, eh?" commented Murphy. "That's a swank
apartment house. This guy got money?"

"I believe he had considerable," replied Warburton, who
ought to have known, since he had paid Hutton large sums
from time to time.

"Have much cash on him when he disappeared?"

"I doubt if he had more than a few hundred."

"A few hundred," remarked the sergeant. "I was on Cape
Cod once. From what I seen of the place a few hundred
would look like a lot of dough to them codfish eaters. You
going to be in town, Mr. Warburton?"

"I'm returning to Cobbport, Massachusetts, this afternoon."

"Oh, well, the Massachusetts cops will get in touch with
you. How about this identifier?"

Warburton rang again. "Have Chase go with this offi-
cer to the morgue to identify a body believed to be Frank
Hutton," he said. "Chase knows him quite well, Mr.
Murphy. Will you go with this young lady?"

"Much obliged," said Murphy who sauntered out in the
wake of the secretary.

It was very clear to William Warburton how his trouble
man had met his death. He had been caught robbing the

house of Stephen Cobb who had murdered him with a blow of his fist and had tossed the body into the sea.

It ought to be easy enough to pin the crime on young Cobb who would have to sell his bonds to secure funds for his defense, but Cobb didn't have to sell them to Warburton. There were half a dozen interests which would pay big money for a chance to wreck the house of William Warburton.

Cobb, after slaying Hutton, had broken into Warburton's residence, in murderous fury. The promoter thumped his desk. Diana as usual was a liar and as usual his jealousy of her had warped his judgment. Cobb, knowing that Warburton had sent Hutton to steal and murder, had come to beat William Warburton to death. He had blundered into the wrong room and Diana, with her natural complacency, had assumed he had come to pay tribute to her charms.

He rose and walked to the window. A great liner with four funnels was moving up the river. Four red funnels. Fifty thousand tons of steel. An irresistible force. That's what he'd be in the case of Steve Cobb. Crush him to powder.

No half measures. No delay. If the police arrested Cobb for murder they would ruin Warburton and Company. He put on his hat and on his way out of the office said to the girl at the information desk:

"I have an engagement which will detain me for some hours. I'll return here for a short time before taking a plane to the Cape."

13

LUCINDA MEETS A CYNIC

"DO YOU MEAN to tell me you are one hundred years old?" exclaimed Lucinda Warburton in a tone of awe.

General Seth Burton grinned and his white porcelains gleamed in the sunlight.

"I told you nothing of the kind," he declared. "I'm a hundred and one years old. I'm old enough to be your great-great-great-grandfather, young woman, and maybe I am, fur all I know. I was a great man with the ladies in my day."

Lucinda giggled. "You're an old sinner," she declared. "But I like you."

"Does my old eyes good to look at you," replied the General gallantly. "As purty a piece as I've seen for many a day. Who's your feller?"

"I haven't any particular fellow," said Lucinda meekly.

"Wall, you grab yourself one quick. Women ain't got much time." He wagged his head sagely.

Miss Warburton, who had encountered the old gentleman abusing the workmen at her beach barrier, had introduced herself and invited him within. They were now sitting on the sand getting acquainted.

"Not much time?" she said perplexedly. "We have as

much time as men. Why I read somewhere that the average woman lives longer than the average man."

"Stuff and nonsense. Oh, I seen old woman that might have been ninety, but they ought to have been dead, being without their faculties. What I mean is that a woman has to catch a man quick fore she withers and dries up into an old maid. How old are you?"

"I'm twenty."

"You ought to have been married long ago. You got mebbe five years."

"Huh," she scowled ferociously and then laughed. "I suppose you were courting girls away back in 1850 when they wore hoopskirts and were afraid to say their souls were their own and married at sixteen and had sixteen children."

"They were well brought up and didn't talk back to their elders," he said significantly.

"The poor miserable things!"

"I married my first wife in 1857. She died in 1870. We had four children. I married my second wife in 1872. Lemme see. I think we had three children. My third woman come along in 1879. She was puny and didn't last long. My fourth wife—let's see, it was in Cleveland's first administration—we didn't have no children."

"I should think not—an old man like you—"

"I was only fifty. It was her fault."

Lucinda laughed derisively.

"Say," said the General complacently, "I could beget children now only I ain't interested in women for a long time. What I mean is I'm a hundred one years old and I know all about the female sex."

"You're a hundred years behind the times," Lucinda

informed him. "Modern women are beautiful till they are fifty and maybe longer and they can marry any time they like, but, if they are smart, they wouldn't be annoyed with men."

"Sez you," sneered the General. "Woman is like a flower. She blooms for a brief time and traps a man and then all she's good for is to produce children."

"You're a horrid old man. You don't know anything. Since the last good looking woman spoke to you, the sex has become the equal of the male and in some respects its superior. There are women judges, congressmen and governors of States but you probably can't read and wouldn't know that."

"I bet you don't even know that women vote."

"I was opposed to that," said the General, "on account there were too many ignorant voters already."

"Women have as good an education as man. They can talk to him on any subject—"

"They always could but they didn't know nothin'," retorted the centenarian. "I've heard of these here educated woman. There was a girl I once knew that cut off her hair and wore men's clothes and was screeching about woman suffrage—lemme see, that was back in the fifties or sixties or along there—I disremember. Her name was Mary Walker. I said to her father—'If you had took a stick to her when she was young, she'd have turned out decent, though mebbe she wouldn't.'"

"You mean Dr. Mary Walker? You mean to say you knew Dr. Mary Walker? Why she was the mother of woman suffrage."

"That's the only kind of mother she was then. Sure I knew her."

"You got lots of notions like these girls that go to college," said the General grimly. "You go get yourself a man quick as you can and have five or six children right away so he's have to scratch to feed and clothe them and won't have no time to chase younger and prettier women. That's the only way to keep a husband. The sexes have been together for thousands of years and ain't changed any 'cept women is getting more brazen. All a woman is good for is to bring up children and that's all she'll ever be good for."

"BUT GENERAL," **PROTESTED** Lucinda, "haven't you heard that a girl swam the English Channel and flew an aeroplane across the Atlantic?"

"Those were old maids that were so homely they were desperate," declared the old fellow. "They only done it to catch a man. Just trying to attract attention to themselves, they were."

"You're incorrigible," she declared angrily. "I'm not trying to catch a man. I wouldn't be annoyed talking to one. I hate men."

General Burton struck at a rock with his stick and cackled sardonically.

"I'm mighty spry," he stated, "and even if I can't read the fine print of newspapers, I can see darn good and my hearing is fine. I seen you making up to Steve Cobb t'other day and you was on the beach crying cause Steve wouldn't marry you, probably."

"Oh!" cried Lucinda. "Oh, you nasty, mean, contemptible old man! How dare you say I want to marry Steve Cobb.

I wouldn't wipe my shoes on him. He's despicable. He's a roue and a libertine."

The old man grinned like a gnome. "That's the kind women like," he said blandly. "Heh, heh, heh. Steve's a lad after my own heart. I was a roue and a libertine and I'm proud of it."

"I was crying because I was angry—he—he was making love to my stepmother. I told him what I thought of him."

"I seen her," said the General. "I seen her like often in my time. She shakes her hips when she walks. First time I seen her come down the Street I sez to myself. 'Jezebel or Salome,' that's what I sez. Helen of Troy was like her and Cleopatra, and Lucrezia Borgia and Lola Montez. I seen Lola Montez out in California. This one is the spit and image of her. A man can tell that kind a mile away if he's a hundred years old like me. No smart man marries them. He makes love to them. Jezebel's the only one that got her just deserts. The dogs ate her up. Don't blame Steve, though. Don't blame him at all. Now, now, baby, don't you cry. Don't listen to a ramblin' old man."

"I'm crying because I hate her so. She's breaking my father's heart. I thank you for the word, Jezebel. That's just what she is."

"The scarlet woman," said the old man gravely. He grinned queerly. "I met lots of them. One of them made me lose millions back in the nineties. Made a fool of me, but I didn't marry her. Courtesans. Lucinda, they have all the best of it. They make their mark on the sands of time, they do. Come to think of it, those kind of women are the only ones in history whose names come down to us. The good women die unsung but the scarlet women live in history."

"That's because men write histories," said Lucinda bitterly.

"Madame Pompadour, Messaline, Sappho—I'm old; I can't remember any more of them."

LUCINDA EYED HIM reflectively. "You are a most amazing old man," she said. "I suspect you're lying about your age, but you are remarkable. And you're right. I'm going to be a famous Courtesan."

"No," said the General. "You ain't the type. Mostly they have red hair and they all have the devil in them. You're a good woman type. You grab yourself a husband."

"What kind of a man is Steve Cobb, really?" demanded Lucinda.

"A fine boy. Just like me at his age."

"Hump. Judging by your confession, you were pretty rotten. Four or five wives and lots of mistresses, no doubt."

"I," said the General proudly, "was a man. I was a soldier and a general, and I fit Indians and, when I saw a woman I wanted, I got her." His mood changed. "And what good did it do? Peace is what a man really needs. Communion with the waves and the wind and the good earth. I'll speak to Steve about you. He might do worse."

"You will, will you?" cried Lucinda, shaking her fist at him. "Don't you dare. If you mention my name to that big idiot, I'll see that you don't live to be a hundred and two."

To her astonishment the old man seemed to crumple and his face was distorted with fear. He lifted his left arm as if to protect his face.

"No, no," he croaked. "You wouldn't hurt a poor old man. I got to live to be a hundred and two. I—I'm afraid to die."

Lucinda stared at him, filled with pity. After all, despite

his amazing lucidity, he was a wretched, doddering creature who had lived a quarter of a century too long.

"I wouldn't hurt you, grandfather, for the world," she said soothingly. "I love you, really I do. I think you'll live to be a hundred fifty."

He laughed, a senile laugh. "Certainly I will," he mumbled. "I'll be the oldest man that ever lived."

She helped him to his feet and conducted him across the barrier, and then with the light of battle in her eye turned toward her home.

"I'm going to have an understanding with that Jezebel," she said aloud through clenched teeth.

14

MYRA GOES THROUGH A WINDOW

MR. AND MRS. BEN SEARS were entertaining visitors in their cottage in Cobbport. The hour was eight in the evening. The Sears had just had their supper which consisted of boiled eggs, borrowed from Steve Cobb, fried fish caught by Ben, hot biscuits, flour lent by Steve Cobb, and tea with cream which Myra had brought home from a visit to Steve early in the evening.

Ben Sears was "on the relief," being a member of the unemployed—permanently unemployed—but he was saying at supper that the New Deal didn't go far enough. Nothing short of an equal distribution among the population of the nation's wealth would suit him, he declared. There ought to be a law against people like Warburton who lived in luxury while decent people couldn't make a living. The Cobbs had been just as bad. He, for one, thought Steve Cobb was getting his just desserts in being broke and having to earn a living like other people. Mr. Sears was talkative because he had a new gallon jug of gin.

As Mrs. Sears pointed out to him frequently enough, they wouldn't have to borrow the necessities of life from their neighbors if Ben would bring home the relief money instead of spending it for liquor. Myra ate silently, occasionally gazing upon her father with a frown of intense dislike.

Ben was a slab-sided, lantern-jawed vacant-eyed man of forty-five who had the Cape Cod equivalent of the Southern hook worm. He was too lazy to go fishing until the larder was completely empty. He affected lumbago when it was desirable to dig a mess of clams. Mostly he spent his days in the shade with several other residents of Cobbport who had anarchistic tendencies.

Mrs. Sears was a very thin, very angular woman with an unattractive face and a disposition which, from years of living with Ben, had soured. She was taciturn by nature. Her ambition was to save enough money to buy a new dress. Myra, who was pretty as a picture, believed, privately, that she didn't belong to these people. She had built up quite a romance about having been stolen from charming and loving parents shortly after birth. Some day, these people who really owned her would drive up in a sixteen cylinder car and take her away from the Ben Sears. Or else Steve Cobb would make a lot of money and marry her, when she got old enough.

Upon the family circle there had intruded without warning Eben Cobb, the Cobbport chief of police, and a round redfaced Irishman introduced as Mr. Noonan, who was a Massachusetts state detective, and who had big hands and feet and a harsh voice, but Myra thought, rather a nice twinkle in his small blue eyes.

Ben Sears, aware of numerous small peculations which might have come home to roost, turned gray when the officers entered, but it was Myra they came to see, not her father.

"Myra," said the Chief, "I want you to tell Mr. Noonan what you told me 'bout Steve Cobb."

Myra grew very white. "Steve hasn't done anything," she protested.

"I ain't said he has," replied the Chief. "It's about the other night when you thought you saw a burglar in his house."

"Why don't you talk to Steve?" she demanded.

"He ain't to home so we come over here, being as Mr. Noonan is in a hurry."

"Well," said Myra, "I was looking out my window and I thought I saw a light in his place and I knew Steve was sleeping out."

"Ah!" exclaimed Mr. Noonan. "And why does he sleep out?"

" 'Cause he likes the open air to sleep in."

"You went up on the hummock where he was asleep and woke him up," prodded the Chief.

SHE NODDED DUBIOUSLY. "And Steve sent me home and that's all I know about it."

"You told me different," declared the Chief.

"Look-a-here, Myra," said her father pompously. "You speak right out. I always thought there was something queer about Steve Cobb."

Mrs. Sears opened her mouth. "Because he's just about fed us for months," she sneered. "Steve's all right and you ought to be ashamed to make insinuations, Ben Sears."

"Steve went down to his house and you sneaked along after him. You heard voices and what sounded like a rumpus, eh?" demanded Eben.

"I was so scared I didn't know what I heard," said Myra, who sensed danger to her hero.

"Then what made you tell me them things?" demanded Eben angrily.

"Don't you talk like that to my daughter!" exclaimed Ben Sears. "Who do you think you are, anyway, you and your tin badge? Go back to your souvenir store and don't come bargin' into the homes of respectable citizens. This is a free country."

"Pipe down," said Noonan harshly. "I'll do the questioning. Now, young woman—"

"Don't you say a word without advice of counsel," shouted her father. "I guess I know my rights."

"Shucks," said Mrs. Sears dryly. "You tell the officers anything you know, Myra. You ain't done anything and neither has Steve Cobb."

"Well," said Myra, "I went over to find out what happened and Steve said there was nobody there and nothing had happened."

"Did you look into the house?" demanded Noonan.

She shook her head. "It was dark. He wouldn't let me come in because it was late so it wasn't proper."

"I demand to know the purpose of this inquiry," this from the head of the family.

"I don't mind telling you," said Noonan.

"A murder has been committed."

"Ooooh," moaned Myra who fell off her chair in a faint. Her father and mother picked her up and carried her into the bedroom.

"She'll be all right," said Noonan who followed them to the bedroom door.

"Leave her lay there. I want some words with you, Mr. Sears."

Mrs. Sears closed the bedroom door and went back to the supper table. The detective reseated himself. Sears folded his arms and struck an attitude.

In the dark of the bedroom, Myra lifted her head from her pillow, planted her feet on the floor and in a second she was through the window and departing from her house at high speed.

A glance told her that Steve's hut was dark. It was too early for him to have gone off with his blanket, so she thought she knew where he was to be found. She went swiftly down to the village. At the farther end of Main Street was the library reading-room, a one-story, three-room house where Steve often spent an evening, glancing over the Boston and New York newspapers.

Looking through the open window, she saw him. He was wearing white duck pants, a sweater and sneakers and he was reading a newspaper. There was nobody else in the reading-room and the librarian was in the other room with her back turned.

"Psst, Steve," she called. He looked up.

"Hello, Princess," he said with his cheerful grin.

"Quick, come out. Something awful has happened."

Steve rose, crossed the room, went out through the door and met her in the street.

"STEVE, DO YOU know anything about a murder?" she demanded tensely.

"Which one? The papers are full of them."

"Down here. That awful Eben Cobb is up there at my house with a State cop and they're asking me all about the night I thought I saw a burglar in your place. When they said there was a murder I fainted, and they put me in my room and I went right out through the window."

"I take it that it was a fake faint," remarked Steve.

"Sure. I had to warn you, didn't I?"

"You precious kid. Do they want to see me?"

"Yes, but I came to warn you to flee for your life."

"I wouldn't think of it, Myra."

She grasped his hand. "Steve, you wouldn't murder anybody, would you?"

"I'm not crazy about the idea," he said.

"Don't worry, Myra. A man named Hutton has disappeared and he was asking for me around the village. I had it all out with Eben, but he must have notified the State police."

"Steve," she said in a frightened tone, "I saw lights in your house and I heard noises and voices. There was somebody there."

"Well, you tell the truth, dear, no matter what happens."

"I said I thought I did," she replied. "That's all I'm going to tell 'em."

He took her hand. "Well, let's go beard the lions, Princess. You and I have clean consciences and right is on our side. You didn't hear voices. You were terribly excited and you thought you did."

"I didn't hear anything," said Myra staunchly. "Oh, Steve, what happened?"

"Nothing of any consequence," he said lightly. "Nothing that bothers me in the slightest degree."

He took the child's hand which was shaking.

"Snap out of it, Myra," he pleaded. "You act guilty."

"I'm so 'fraid for you, Steve. That Mr. Noonan has awful sharp eyes. Did you—did you—"

"My conscience is as clear as a glass of water, dear. You go home, sneak back into your room and I'll light my lamp. When they see the light in my house they'll call on me."

"Well, I s'pose it's all right if you say so."

However, when the pair turned into the lane leading toward the residences of both Steve and Myra, they encountered the officers coming down the narrow road.

"That's him," cried Eben excitedly. "She went and warned him, just as I said."

"That makes her accessory after the fact."

15

AN ARREST AND A RESCUE

"EBEN," SAID STEVE sternly, "another crack like that and I'll pull your whiskers out by the roots. Go home, Myra, and let me talk to these people. Scamper, now."

"Your name Stephen Cobb?"

"Sure. What's yours?" said Steve cheerfully.

"William Noonan, Massachusetts State officer. I've business with you."

"Come up to my humble home," requested Cobb. "You can come, too, Eben. Go to bed, Myra."

"Look here, Steve Cobb, I'm Chief of Police of this here town and don't you forget it. You can't threaten me with impunity, you can't," blustered Eben Cobb. "Myra, you go home and stay there. We got to ask you more questions and you better not pretend to faint next time."

Myra was weeping. Steve patted her shoulder kindly and pushed her along the lane ahead of him. Noonan fell into step by his side.

"Don't you be frightened, little girl," the officer said kindly. "We won't bother you any more."

Leading the way into his domicile, Steve lighted the lamp and invited his visitors to seat themselves.

Myra lingered a short distance away, but, hearing no disturbance within, finally trotted homeward.

"You're the fellow who was a champion weight lifter and hammer thrower and wrestler and boxer in college," said Noonan, who eyed Cobb's proportions admiringly. "You're the son of Ezra Cobb who owned the Cobb Company."

"I wasn't a champion in all those events," said Steve modestly, "but I was pretty good. And my father was Ezra Cobb."

"You could kill a man with a blow of your fist, I expect," said the officer thoughtfully.

"Oh, I'm mild and gentle as a lamb," replied Steve. "What's the cause of this visitation?"

"We're trying to find out who murdered Frank Hutton."

Steve lifted his eyebrows. "Eben told me that a man named Hutton had disappeared. Was he murdered?"

"He was."

Steve felt a gripe in his stomach, but his face did not betray his feeling.

"We have good reason to believe that Hutton called on you the night of his death."

"Indeed!"

"We know you had a fracas with somebody up here that night."

"You seem to be well-informed," said Steve dryly.

"Suppose you make a clean breast of it?" suggested the detective.

"You make me laugh," retorted Steve.

"Okay, feller. Hutton was sent to see you by Mr. Warburton, who is now owner of the Cobb Company, on some business matter. Hutton inquired of a man at the gas station where you lived. The Sears girl saw a light in your house. She went up on that hill back there and woke you up. You came down to investigate, the girl heard voices and a rumpus. She came to the door. The light was out and you told her that nobody had been here."

"Yes, I told her that. She was sure there was a burglar. She was excited. I sent her home to bed."

"Next day the Chief came up here. He found, in your ash barrel, broken glass and articles which had been smashed in this fight. He found a bullet imbedded in your frame."

"He told me all that."

"Yet you say there was nobody here."

"I don't own a revolver, Mr. Noonan. A shot would awaken the town. That bullet may have been in the door-frame for years."

"No, it was recent. I examined the hole. It was clean and new. Things look bad for you, Cobb."

"Look here," said Steve earnestly. "I have no money and no valuables. This hut speaks for itself. I didn't know this Hutton. I would have no reason to attack him. It would amuse me to find a burglar in this place. And, as Hutton seems to be a friend of Warburton's, it's most unlikely that he would rob my house."

"Hutton was killed by a terrific blow on the temple such as a man of your strength could deliver," said Noonan.

"But what would be my motive?"

"The motive will turn up."

"May I ask, if this man has disappeared, how you know he was killed at all and particularly how you know the manner in which he was killed?"

"Because we have the body," said Noonan quietly. Steve's eyes almost stuck out of his head and his mouth opened.

"I—I don't believe you," he muttered.

"No, of course you don't. And why? Because you threw him into the sea," shouted Noonan who whipped a revolver from his pocket and covered Steve Cobb with it. "And the revenue boat, Tecumseh, picked him up. Oh, we have the body and there ain't any doubt in the world we have the murderer.

"Here, Chief," he added, as he fished with his left hand a pair of handcuffs from his pocket. "Put these bracelets on him."

STEVE ROSE. STANDING four feet from the table he blew out the lamp, plunging the room into darkness. He dropped flat as a bullet tore out of the gun and whined above him.

"Grab him," shouted Eben Cobb. Steve's big arm shot out, grasped the Chief by both knees, and pulled him over. Noonan came charging like a bull afraid to fire in the dark for fear of hitting his fellow officer. Steve crouched on his knees, caught the detective, as he came in, with a back breaking grip about the middle, dodged a blow with the butt of the gun and tore it from his hand, tossed it to a corner of the room and came back to sanity.

"All right, boys," he said. "I'll light the lamp. I just don't let any darn fool pull a gun on me. I surrender voluntarily. You haven't a damn thing on me and you know it."

"Now you're talking sense, confound you," mumbled Noonan. "Where's my gun?"

Steve was up and fumbling for matches. He had hurled Noonan in the direction of the couch. He had been shocked out of his self-control when informed that the body of Hutton had been picked up and, for a second, had yielded to the natural impulse of the guilty man to make his get-away. But he'd have to fight this thing, tell the truth and hope he would persuade a jury that his homicide was justifiable.

"This won't do you any good, you know," growled Noonan. "Eh?"

For the room was suddenly filled with men. They were outlined as they plunged through the doorway, four or five of them. A flashlight covered Steve Cobb with golden rays, blinding him momentarily. It showed Noonan on his feet at the sofa, Eben Cobb still crouching on the floor.

"Grab the big fellow," cried somebody hoarsely. "Hands up, you others."

And Steve's fury burst again. He couldn't resist the law, but he found men in front of him upon whom he could vent the despair and rage and self-contempt with which he was filled. With a roar, he plunged at the holder of the flashlight which immediately went out. And for a minute or two there raged a battle royal in the dark in which fists and feet whirled and struck flesh; in which there were grunts and curses and heavy breathing. Noonan was in the fray, both arms swinging like flails, and Steve's huge fists were crashing against chests and faces. In the narrow precincts it was impossible for a fist to miss a target. Once Steve received a crushing blow on the shoulder from a blackjack.

"Crack."

There was a sharp report from a revolver and a groan. In the illumination afforded by the gun flash, Steve floored the man who had fired it. And then something heavy descended upon his head.

"Got him," said a triumphant voice. "Let's go. Pick him up and carry him."

Fighting ceased. Four men lifted the heavy weight which was Steve Cobb and bore him out of the house and down the lane.

They encountered no one.

At the foot of the lane stood an open touring car, a chauffeur behind the wheel. They dropped the body of Steve Cobb in the bottom of the tonneau and piled in.

16

THE GREEN YAWL

STEVE COBB CAME back to consciousness in a row boat. He was lying in the bottom. He sat up abruptly and was pushed back even more abruptly, but he had seen something. He was not in Cobbport Haven—he could tell that at a glance, even at night. But the rowboat was close alongside a yacht and it was a green yawl—the same which had been swinging at its moorings in Cobbport that afternoon.

A man in the bow of the boat caught a line tossed from the yawl, and the little craft was drawn alongside. Steve was pulled to his haunches, the muzzle of a gun thrust between his shoulder blades.

"How about going up under your own steam," a voice suggested.

Steve had a headache, not to be wondered at since he had breathed deeply of the fumes of chloroform after being cracked on the head with a blackjack, and he was somewhat confused, but things were beginning to clear up. He climbed to his feet and went up the ladder. Two armed men stood on deck and four followed him on board.

"Down below," said a voice behind him, Steve descended into the same cabin in which he had interrupted a love scene, but he was urged across it down a narrow companionway and steered to a stateroom with a tiny porthole. The door was slammed shut behind him and locked, and Steve threw himself upon the bunk with a sigh of weariness. A moment later the yawl quivered and shook, which meant she had a gas engine auxiliary and was under way.

After a moment he rose, fumbled until he found the electric light button, ran water in the wash stand and soaked his head. Immediately he felt better.

For purposes unknown to him, Jack Clews, the yachts-man had landed with his crew and forcibly rescued him from the officers of the law. He was now being taken to sea.

Where was the yawl bound? She certainly wasn't going to cross the ocean so she must be headed for Nantucket, one of the islands at the mouth of Buzzard's Bay or some infrequented Cape Inlet. Why had the yachtsmen inter-fered with his arrest? What did they want of Steve Cobb? Whatever they wanted, they wouldn't get it!

Unfortunately, it would appear to the police as though he had been a party to the attack on State officer Noonan and the local Chief of Police; that he was a member of the gang which had come to his rescue. And his original atti-tude when Noonan ordered him handcuffed would bear that out.

Steve saw clearly that Noonan had very little upon which to accuse him of killing Hutton. Warburton, of course, had set the police on him, and was unlikely to supply them with a motive—the bonds. He would have been careful not to mention them. They would have been unable to prove that he had ever met the dead man; they had no witnesses who had seen them together in the hut—why they couldn't convict him in a million years. Therefore these rascals had

done him an ill turn in forcibly taking him from the officers.

It was a most unfortunate thing that Hutton's body had
been recovered but, if Steve had only taken the precaution
of emptying his victim's pockets, it was most unlikely that
the man would have been identified.

Never having killed anybody before, his technique in
disposing of the body had been very faulty.

The question now was why Jack Clews had interfered.
Was it possible that Clews had the bonds and had to put
their owner out of the way before he made use of them?

That wasn't likely. As Steve was towing the body of
Hutton to sea, Mrs. Warburton had rowed out to this
yawl. Three hours later she was still on board, drinking and
making merry with the yachtsman. The bonds had been
stolen between his departure from the hut with the trouble
man and his return without him.

He sat down on the edge of the bunk unable to make
head or tail out of the situation. Ten minutes passed and
he stiffened. The key was turning in the lock. The door
opened and there appeared upon the threshold the last
person in the world he expected to find on board—the
dashing and effulgent Mrs. Warburton. She wore a white
costume which made her jet black hair the more alluring.
She smiled upon him ironically.

"Hello, Tarzan," she said brightly.

Steve thrust his fingers through his thick light hair. His
expression must have been comical because she laughed
gaily. She came into the room and stood in front of him.

"Move over," she commanded. "Glad to see me, lover?"

"Can that stuff," he growled but he moved over. She

seated herself beside him on the edge of the bunk. Her right arm went over his shoulder. Steve removed it.

"NONE OF THAT," he said angrily. "Are you responsible for what's happened?"

"And how," she boasted. "Aren't you surprised?"

"You must be crazy."

"I am. Crazy about you." She snuggled against him. She reminded him of a beautiful Persian cat but a wild one.

He eyed her speculatively. If he throttled her, carried her on deck as a shield, what were his prospects of getting ashore? Slight. The yawl suddenly lurched as a sizable sea struck her. They were well out in the Sound.

"Suppose you explain what it's all about," he said less truculently.

"Of course," she agreed with a brilliant smile. "You should be very grateful to me because I'm your guardian angel. You were about to be robbed and murdered. Thanks to me you are safe upon a very comfortable yacht and I hope you are grateful."

"Then your intentions are benevolent," he inquired. "I am knocked senseless and then chloroformed by a bunch of thugs and it was all in my best interests."

"Jack says there was no time to explain; that you were battling with my husband's ruffians and you assumed that he and his crew were reenforcements. I hope you weren't badly hurt, darling."

He grinned. "I can stand a lot of hard usage, Mrs. Warburton. So they were hirelings of your husband, eh? May I ask how and why you figure in the affair."

"But I'm going to tell you everything, Steve. I've always

loathed my husband. I have even more reason for hating him than you have—"

"I'm not interested—"

"You are. Listen. I was in love with a man and Warburton ruined him and drove him to suicide. I didn't find out the truth until I had married Warburton and I've remained with him waiting for an opportunity to destroy him. Oh, I could have divorced him but that wasn't enough. I had to crush him."

"Well but—"

"Listen to me. I've spied on William, I've steamed open his private correspondence, listened at key holes, read his telegrams, vamped his agents—Hutton for instance—I've stopped at nothing—"

"Rather despicable. Please don't paw me."

"You'll learn to like it, my dear. I'll tell you something you don't know. Your father died of slow poisoning—I can't prove it but I know it. Stop—you hurt me."

For Steve had grasped her by the shoulder and his nails were cutting into her soft flesh.

"How do you know?" he cried fiercely.

"I got it out of Hutton."

"I was listening the night my husband and Hutton discussed you and your bonds. There is a little room off the library with an exit into the hall and the partition between it and the library is very thin—"

"You telling me?" demanded Steve. "My father had it built as a bar for service in the library."

"Well I heard William say that if he could get rid of you and get the bonds he could retire them as of six months back and float his new stock. At the time I didn't know

Steve tossed Clews heavily upon the deck.

who you were or where you lived, but I determined to find you and warn you."

"So you went out to the yawl," said Steve ironically.

"I HAD PROMISED to see Jack Clews. He's connected with interests opposed to my husband, but he's a good friend of mine. He got drunk and disorderly that night, as you know. After you left, I told him what I had learned and he agreed to get in touch with his principals in New York and make you a proposition."

"Humph. Why do you suppose I broke into your house that night?"

"Well, I'd had too much champagne. I'm afraid I didn't reason very clearly."

"What do you think now?" he asked anxiously.

"I suppose you had killed Hutton, after learning that my

husband sent him and came to murder my husband. You give the impression of being very primitive."

"I am."

"That's why I'm crazy about you," she cried. "Steve, Clews wants to help you."

Her vehemence was convincing. "All right," he said. "Why didn't you have Clews call on me and make a proposition? Why kidnap me like a rich man's baby?"

"There was no time. Everything happened at once. William flew back from New York tonight. At seven o'clock a man came to see him. They were closeted in the library for half an hour. I listened in the little room.

"This man is a New York criminal. It seems Hutton's body has been found and identified. You were going to be arrested. Tonight, the man who came to see my husband was going to go to your house with others and pass themselves off as officers and take you to New York. My husband intended to make you turn over your bonds in exchange for your liberty. He said your arrest would do him more harm than good.

"I rowed out to the yawl and enlisted Jack Clews. He landed some of his crew and had the yawl drop down to Falmouth. They brought you here in a motor car. You owe your liberty and, perhaps, your life to me."

"Much obliged," he said dryly. "So what?"

"Well, you ought to love me a little."

"Mrs. Warburton, you're a very beautiful woman but I'm not in the mood for sentiment. I take it I'm to sell my bonds to Clews and his gang."

"There will be money enough for all of us," she assured him.

"Well, I'll have to think it over. I'm tired. I've been drugged and beaten up. Does Clews know who the men were who were in my house?"

"What does it matter?"

"Quite a little. They were really police. They had just placed me under arrest."

He grinned to see Diana grow pale.

"Suppose you leave me alone. I've got to think," he suggested.

"Yes, yes, of course." Mrs. Warburton at the moment was so shocked at his information that her amatory desires, real or feigned, had oozed away. Running foul of the law was not palatable to her and she was eager to consult with her confederates.

"Get a good night's sleep," she advised him. "We'll meet at breakfast."

He gazed somberly at the door she had closed behind her but which she had forgotten to lock.

The police! Warburton's hirelings and Clews and his gang. Three outfits lined up against him. And a fourth element was in possession of the bonds.

Diana Warburton had burned her bridges when she left her husband's house and sailed off on the yawl. She couldn't go back. What would she say and do when she learned Steve didn't have the bonds? Refuse to believe him, of course.

CLEWS HAD STEPPED outside the law. His wrath, when he found he had failed to gain by it, would be formidable. Most likely they would think he was holding out on them and they'd try force to make him disgorge.

He opened the door and stepped into the companionway. He walked down to the cabin where Diana was sitting in earnest conference with Clews.

Clews grinned at him and waved his hand.

"No hard feelings, old top," he said cordially.

Steve grinned back. "On the contrary, I'm obliged to you. They were about to handcuff me."

Clews looked concerned. "Diana has been telling me. Are you sure they weren't Warburton's men?"

"Real officers. State police officer Noonan and the chief of police of Cobbport."

"I think one of them was shot," said Clews somberly. "You going to come in with us?"

"What else can I do?" replied Steve. "Mind if I go on deck? I need fresh air. If you'd told me who you were, you wouldn't have had to drug me."

"Sit down. I want to talk to you," commanded the yawl owner.

Steve seated himself opposite the pair.

"Cobb," said the broker, "you're in a hell of a hole. You stand a swell chance of going to the electric chair for murder. You can thank me that you're not in the County jail at this minute."

"I can take care of myself," said Steve curtly. He had not cared for Clews at their first meeting and he liked him less now. Clews was an artificially youthful man, meaning that an active life and a fondness for yachting gave him muscles and good health and appearance of being ten years younger than his probable forty-five. But the fellow had a heavy nose and small deep set eyes and a brutal mouth.

"Just what did you propose to do with your bonds?" he demanded.

"I hadn't made any plans."

"You intended to let him put out his securities and then prosecute him criminally, eh?"

"That," said Steve brightly, "is an idea."

"I've a better one. You've plenty of reason for being sore at Warburton but the only thing worth while in life is money. Prosecute him and the bond issue will flop, Warburton's firm will go to the wall and there will be slim pickings. Now we'll take a different tack—"

"Pardon me, did I understand you to say 'we?'" inquired Steve blandly.

Clews grinned. "Sure. I'm declaring myself in. We hold him up. We sell him the bonds for two and a half million dollars which is absolutely all the traffic will bear. We split is three ways, you, I, and Diana here. If it weren't for this girl, you'd have made a sap play and nobody would have profited."

"Why should I take you into partnership?" inquired Steve.

"Because you've got to. You're on board my boat. My crew is loyal. You saw how they battled for me at your house. I'll take you to a safe place and open negotiations with Warburton in your name. You'll do exactly as I say, sign what I tell you to, and take your cut and like it."

"Suppose I don't like taking orders."

"You big goof, you've got to. I'm your only hope. You killed Hutton, you've escaped the police, you're a hunted man."

"MRS. WARBURTON," SAID Steve. "I thought you wanted to ruin your husband. Mr. Clews' proposition will enable him to remain in business."

"Well," said Diana, smiling broadly, "two and a half millions are not to be sneezed at."

"You've got me," said Steve to Clews, "but how are you going to get the bonds?"

"I'm not worrying about that," said Clews rising and approaching Steve Cobb.

"With the bonds in your possession, you can make me sign them over and then you won't need me," said Steve thoughtfully. "And as I'm a fugitive from justice, nobody would weep if I were found dead somewhere."

He gazed sharply at Clews and saw in the mean eyes that he had struck home.

"Old man," said Clews genially. "I don't work like that. Let's shake and call it a deal." He extended his hand. Steve grasped it, whirled, swung Clews over his back and tossed him heavily upon the deck.

Mrs. Warburton opened her mouth and screamed at the top of her lungs. Clews, with an oath, pulled a revolver from his pocket but Steve tore it from his hand. He smashed his rubber-soled shoe into the broker's face, darted up the hatchway and encountered three seamen coming at a run.

"Stand back," he bellowed lifting the revolver. The sailors stopped in their tracks. With a wild laugh, Steve Cobb rushed to the rail, soared over it, dropping the weapon as he plunged toward the water, and hit cleanly, his arms above his head. He dove deep, swam under water for some distance and came to the surface at last to see the yawl merging into the shadows, her port light gleaming like a red star.

There was commotion on the yacht and somebody fired a revolver blindly at the sea, six shots. He chuckled. There was no moon and he doubted if the yawl had a search light. Her prospects of picking him up were exceedingly slight. Nevertheless she was going to try. Presently he saw her starboard light which meant that she had come about.

He could afford to ignore her. He slipped out of his trousers, kicked off his sneakers, pulled his sweater over his head and began to swim easily. The sea was his friend and companion; on the northern horizon was a line of lights five or six miles away, the Cape Cod shore. There wasn't the slightest doubt in his mind that he could make it.

Knowing the currents and entirely at home in a choppy sea, he assumed he would land ten or fifteen miles east of Cobbport and once ashore he would find a quick way home.

Steve hadn't gone overboard to escape the wrath of Clews. He wasn't afraid of Clews and his crew—he was more afraid of the advances of the unprincipled Mrs. Warburton. He doubted very much whether Clews had nerve enough to do more than bluster and threaten. Without the bonds, the death of Steve Cobb would be of no use to Clews. The trouble was that the fellow would hold him captive and there were things Steve had to do.

THE BONDS HAD been held in trust for him and delivered to him upon his twenty-first birthday by the Mammouth Trust Company of New York. His ownership of them was unquestioned. It had been absurd for Pennypacker to declare that he should have turned them over with the rest of the Cobb securities when his father made his settlement. His father had been a sick man and Steve had had nothing to do with the arrangement between Ezra Cobb and Warburton.

He had hesitated to advertise for them as lost or stolen because he had hoped to recover them, but now he would insert advertisements in Boston and New York papers, describing them fully, and that effectually would block a sale of them to Warburton by the thief.

He would hide out in Cobbport and he knew plenty of hiding places, until he had a chance to settle with Warburton whom he had no doubt was his father's murderer. There was a streak of the primitive in Steve. As he swam with lusty strokes, he was considering the advisability of strangling Warburton with his bare hands and paying the penalty.

The advertisements would block both Warburton's game and Clews. He had no money but it would only take a small sum and he thought he knew where he could get it. General Burton, the centenarian. He knew that the monthly pension check had arrived only a few days ago. Back to Cobbport, up to Boston to insert the ads, back again to Cobbport for an interview with Warburton and then let State Officer Noonan do his worst.

Death by slow poisoning. No wonder Ezra Cobb had faltered, made grave errors of judgment, lost his fighting heart, surrendered to his enemy and then died.

Steve underestimated the time it would take him to reach the shore. More than three hours and a half had passed before he touched bottom upon a pebble beach and waded out upon dry land. Most of the shore lights had been extinguished as the inhabitants of the shore cottages had retired. He found himself on a rough part of the beach at a considerable distance from any settlement. He was leg and arm weary but not winded. He estimated that he was somewhere between Hyannis and Chatham and a good fifteen miles from Cobbport.

It was a bit chilly, too, for a person who had burned up a lot of vitality in the ocean and who was clad only in narrow trunks. He climbed over a rail fence and found himself in a meadow. If there were habitations in the vicinity they were unlighted and so invisible. When halfway across the meadow, however, he heard ahead the roar of a rapidly moving motor car and a few seconds later saw the beams of a pair of headlights. The State road was only a hundred yards away which was a source of satisfaction.

A moment later Steve climbed another rail fence, hopped a ditch and stood upon paved road. It would take him a good five hours to walk to Cobbport.

17

TRAPPED

BY THAT TIME it would be daylight and it wouldn't be exactly safe for Steve Cobb to be seen in daylight in Cobbport after what had happened this evening. He hadn't the time to walk to Cobbport.

He set out however and had walked a quarter of a mile when he saw a pair of yellow eyes come over a slight rise half a mile away. At this hour there was no chance of a car stopping for a pedestrian who thumbed it, particularly a naked pedestrian.

Steve lay down in the middle of the road. He lay like one dead, though every muscle was tense, every sense alert. The motor car approached at fifty miles an hour. Its lights illumined the road for a hundred yards ahead of it. They flashed suddenly upon the huge bronzed body of the recumbent person in the road. The horn honked. Then brakes screeched. The car came on more slowly. Steve clenched his hands. If it didn't stop in time he would try to roll out of its path, but he might roll too late.

He was bathed in its illumination. It was only a few rods away. It was stopping. It had stopped. Its bumper was only twenty feet away from him.

"Hey, there," somebody shouted.

No response. There was the sound of a door slamming. Through half closed eyes Steve saw a man in a chauffeur's uniform approaching cautiously.

"What's the matter?" a woman screamed from the car.

"Looks like a dead man," said the man. He stood over Steve Cobb. Suddenly Steve Cobb rose up and as he rose, his right fist lifted faster. It caught the chauffeur on the point of the jaw. The woman in the car shrieked.

Steve ran swiftly to the side of the machine as the chauffeur replaced him as a motionless form on the paving. He peered in. There was a red headed girl in the front seat of a roadster who wore a white nurse's uniform under a light tan coat. Steve pulled open the door.

"Get out," he said harshly, "and look after your boy friend."

With a wail of terror, the girl darted past him, leaped into the road and ran toward the unconscious chauffeur. Steve was in the driver's seat in a jiffy. He stepped on the starter, threw the machine into reverse, ran back twenty or thirty yards and turned the car around. By this time the chauffeur was up and rushing toward the machine uttering furious oaths.

Steve laughed wildly, threw the machine into high gear and in a moment was proceeding toward Cobbport in an expensive high-powered car at seventy miles an hour. He had solved the problem of transportation. For a man charged with murder, the accusation of stealing a car was a trifle.

Chauffeur and nurse had been out joyriding in their employer's automobile. Steve hoped they wouldn't have far to walk and that they wouldn't be fired as a result of their escapade, but he had more important things to think about.

The difference between fifteen minutes and three hours might mean everything in the world to him. He slowed up passing through villages for he had no desire to attract the attention of speed cops, but in the open he pushed her up to eighty miles an hour. And in about a quarter of an hour he drew up in the outskirts of Cobbport, turned the machine into a side road and abandoned it, as he supposed, temporarily.

He walked boldly into the village which might have been a cemetery for all the life it displayed. It was a soft balmy night, the south wind carrying warmth from the Gulf stream. The General lived in a two story cottage not far from the fishing pier. It was quite likely that he would be awake and he might even be wandering along the shore or squatting on the pebbles watching the rippling waves and thinking of something that happened in his boyhood.

As Steve reached the shore he saw riding lights at the yawl's moorings while the breeze wafted to his ears across the still harbor the sound of rowlocks.

The yawl had returned and Mrs. Warburton was going home. "What a nerve, what a nerve," Steve chuckled. "And how like the woman!" Her plot having failed, the lady was returning to the bosom of her family. If Warburton saw her come in she would brazen it out as she had brazened out the presence of Steve Cobb in her room. She certainly was the financier's weak spot.

DIANA DID NOT propose to desert her husband for a trifle of alimony. With Cobb and his bonds, she could rook Warburton for all he owned; without them she might as well go back and wait for another opportunity. The boat was moving toward the Warburton landing and presently its rowlocks were silent. Did she suppose Steve had been fool enough to commit suicide?

She ought to know that a fellow like him could swim five or six miles and think nothing of it.

He ought to follow her into the house, drag Warburton out of his bed and let him have what he had given poor old Ezra Cobb.

However, Steve's blood had had time to cool. Murderer or not, he couldn't take justice into his own hands. It was one thing to protect his property with his giant strength, but it had been an accident that he had killed Hutton.

He pushed open the door of the General's house, found the matches—he knew its interior as well as his own—and lighted one.

The place was empty but the bed had been occupied. The old fellow, unable to sleep, often wandered about for hours in the stilly night.

Steve knew where he kept his hoard, but great as was his need, he couldn't touch it without permission. He went out of the house and began to reconnoitre the shore carefully working toward the Warburton estate. It was so dark, nevertheless, that he would have passed the brooding old man if the General hadn't lifted his cracked voice.

"That you Steve Cobb?" he demanded.

"General, I was looking for you."

He went over and seated himself beside the old fellow.

"Couldn't sleep," said the old man.

"Worried about you, Steve."

"I thought you never worried," replied the youth.

"Ain't had no cause for years and years. Steve, the wages of sin is death—if they catch you."

The General had his back against a big rock at a spot where the road to Warburton's came within thirty feet of the beach.

"I've heard that," said Steve grimly.

"They're looking for you Steve. They'll electrocute you sure as shooting."

"I don't think so, General."

"But you killed that fellow. I saw you packing him into the sea."

"You're not going to testify against me, I hope?"

"Not me," said the General. "Why didn't you let him rob you, Steve? You didn't have nothing."

"You're mistaken," replied Steve. "I had some very valuable bonds in a card board box tucked away on a rafter."

"You had? Then it was all a bluff 'bout being a convert to the wind and the sea."

"Not exactly, General. Aside from the bonds, I had nothing and there were reasons why I couldn't do anything with them. In a year or two maybe, I might have righted a great wrong with them. In the meantime I enjoyed life here and having you for a friend."

"Well you got 'em back. You killed the robber and got 'em back. Don't see why they're making a fuss about a housebreaker."

"I prevented him from taking them. I put them back in their hiding place and carried Hutton out into the middle of the Sound.

"I was gone about three hours. When I returned the bonds had been taken. I could find them nowhere."

"Wall I swan! What made you keep val'ables in a place like that?"

"I was a fool. There never was a thief in Cobbport—not until Warburton came to live here."

"By gosh!" cried the general excitedly.

"Jezebel."

"What on earth are you talking about?"

"She goes round half naked, she does and she shakes her hips like a wanton."

"Rather an apt description of Mrs. Warburton," said Steve dryly.

"THAT'S HER. STEVE, I seen you packing that corpse into the sea and I sat there and thought about it. I knew you wouldn't do no wrong, so you must have a reason. I wasn't going to give you away nohow."

"You mean Lucinda Warburton?"

"Sure. Her and me are comrades." He cackled shrilly. "We fit like nobody's business, but that's all right. She thinks a lot of you, Steve."

"Yes," he said bitterly, "she acts like it."

There was a silence. The General had lost himself and couldn't remember what he had been talking about.

"You said something about Jezebel," said Steve absently. He was wondering how to broach the subject of a small loan. He had a few hundred dollars in the county bank, but he couldn't present himself to draw any of it. Why of course—the General would cash a check for thirty or forty dollars.

"Jezebel?" Let's see. Oh yes. Maybe she took them bonds."

"I happen to know that the lady was keeping a date out

on the green yawl. She boarded it as I was swimming out of the harbor and she was on board when I returned."

"That's all you know," said the General with a triumphant titter. "I'm a settin' down near the boat landing when a rowboat ties up and out comes this woman with her neck and bosom bare and a man with a yachting cap. They come right toward me and they was going to step on me when I sung out to them.

"Yes. Go on."

"Where was I? Oh, yes. The man asks me if I know where Steve Cobb lived, so I walk a piece with them and point out your house.

" 'He lives there, but he ain't to home,' I tells 'em."

"Jezebel says, 'Oh, then we can't call.' "

" ' It ain't no hour to go callin', specially without no clothes on,' " I tells her straight out. She laughs fit to kill herself, the hussy. 'Well, let's go up to my house,' she says and they start down the street so I go back to the shore. 'Bout half an hour afterwards who comes down to the boat but her and him, but this time they don't see me. I bet they stole your bonds, Steve. I wouldn't put anything past her."

Steve drew a long breath. What had been a mystery had been explained. He had been at sea three hours. Plenty of time for the pair to return to the yawl and celebrate their achievement by getting intoxicated.

He had not the slightest doubt that Clews and Mrs. Warburton were the thieves. Diana had listened in the ancient bar to the conference in the library between Hutton and Warburton—she had confessed that. She had gone out to the yawl as soon as she could get away. No doubt she had not expected that Hutton would go to Steve Cobb's house so soon. The pair had decided to forestall Warburton and secure the bonds which, in the wrong hands, would ruin him. And they had landed and paid a call while Steve was towing Hutton's body out to sea.

That explained why they had wrecked the place. They had no notion where to find the securities and probably had discovered them by accident. And it explained a queer silence when he told them his name after going on board the yawl on his return.

HAVING THE BONDS, of course, they needed him. That was why Mrs. Warburton had taken advantage of his appearance in her room, why she had wished her husband to think he was visiting her clandestinely while she knew he had come for the missing bonds.

And, without him, the securities could not be used. Which was the reason for his abduction. He shivered. On that yawl he had been in more deadly peril than he knew. He couldn't see a man like Clews giving a third of two and a half millions to anybody. Most likely he would cheat Diana out of her share of the spoils.

So the bonds were on the yawl. And the yawl was out there in the harbor.

"Why in hell didn't you tell me this days ago?" he demanded angrily.

The general winced. "I didn't want you to worry, Steve. I didn't s'pose you had anything worth stealin'. And, I guess I kind of forgot."

"Well, you've certainly done me a favor by remembering. Listen."

He heard the sound of a motor car coming from the direction of Warburton's.

The General stood up. "Pretty late for them to be fooling

round," he muttered. "Mebbe that's Jezebel running away with what belongs to you, Steve." He moved out into the road just as automobile headlights rounded a curve and came into play. The old man stood in the road lifting his stick like an amateur traffic policeman.

Instead of slowing up, the car increased speed.

"Come back here, you old fool," shouted Steve.

The General decided to be discreet and backed to the roadside still bathed in the lights. It was an open touring car with several people in it. And, as it passed a female voice was lifted.

"General, help, help, it's Lucin—" the voice was choked off. Steve had a glimpse of three or four men and a small form wrapped in a black coat with a man's hat pulled down over the eyes.

"Steve," wailed the centenarian. "It's Lucinda. They're carrying her off."

He shook his stick impotently at the rear of the car. Steve Cobb was already rushing down the shore at top speed. He saw the car swing left just outside the village. It would hit the main road in a mile and turn north or south. If it turned south it would arrive eventually at the jumping-off place which is Provincetown. If it turned north, it had twenty miles to go before the road forked for Boston and inland points.

He rushed into the General's house, grasped the wallet out of the bottom bureau drawer, bounded the few hundred yards to his own hut, risking the presence of an officer awaiting his return. There was no one there. He snatched a sweater, duck pants and a pair of shoes and without stopping to put them on, tore through the village street toward the point where he had abandoned the stolen car.

18

PURSUIT OF LUCINDA

THEY WERE MILES ahead of him, of course, but the road was straight with no turn-offs. He got into his sweater as he ran, pulled on the pants, at the side of the car, thrust the wallet into the pocket, pulled on the shoes, jammed his foot on the starter and was off in pursuit. The stolen car had plenty of power and was capable of high speed. Steve gave it all it would take and the needle passed seventy when he straightened out on the highway.

He was unarmed and he didn't care. Lucinda Warburton was nothing to him. It would serve his enemy right, if his daughter were carried off by kidnapers. He was a fugitive from justice, himself, charged with murder. He was driving a stolen car. But his jaw was set, his eyes were gleaming, he was muttering savagely as he tore through the night.

Lucinda was nothing to him. His enemy's daughter. Daughter of the man who had sent Hutton to kill him, who was responsible for the horrible predicament he was in. Back on the yawl were his bonds which were to be the instrument of his vengeance. He ought to be boarding the yawl instead of chasing armed bandits without a weapon. He tried to make the car go faster than she would.

Lucinda was nothing to him except a face that was

always before him; petulant, proud, sweet and gallant. His lips still tasted that first and only kiss. He would tear these rats limb from limb, when he caught up with them. Damn them!

On through the night. A motor car coming the other way honked reprovingly and then dipped into the ditch to give the madman room.

Mile after mile and no sign of a tail light. Five miles, ten miles, twenty miles and through Buzzard's Bay Village. Not far north the road divided.

Cheated out of their job by the gang from the yawl, the criminals brought over by Warburton to capture Steve Cobb had returned to Warburton who had refused to pay them their price. In revenge they had broken into the house and carried off the rich man's daughter.

It wasn't the first time there had been a kidnaping on Cape Cod but the previous one was just the work of amateurs. That beautiful little creature in the hands of thugs! Steve had heard the inside of several "snatches." When the victim was a beautiful young woman, things were apt to happen to her, ransom or no ransom. He snarled with fury at the thought of lewd hands on the girl who despised him and whom he had scorned because of her father.

No tail light in sight and in less than a minute he would be at the fork in the highroads. These were New Yorkers. Warburton knew who they were. The pursuit would be in the direction of New York so they would take the road for Plymouth and Boston.

He went east on two wheels and tore along the road above the Cape Cod canal. A police whistle had sounded back there when he roared across the drawbridge. He couldn't bother about that.

THERE WERE HILLS now which the car skimmed over as though they were on level ground. And when he turned, at Sandwich, into a long straightaway, he saw, miles ahead, a winking red light.

Driving with his left hand at seventy miles an hour, he pulled up the seat beside him and groped. He came up with a car jack, a heavy hunk of metal weighing at least twenty pounds. He was not gaining on the kidnapers.

The light kept at the same distance ahead and his car could do no more.

All of a sudden, he began to gain rapidly. It was incredible. No, it was true. The car ahead had stopped. Steve slowed down. Mustn't let them think he was pursuing them. In a minute his headlights picked up the car which was at the roadside. Two men were changing a rear tire. He became aware, suddenly, that, miles back, there were a pair of headlights. Police or tardy travelers.

He slowed to thirty. The jack lay beside him on the seat. Two men were sitting in the rear seat of the other car. No sign of Lucinda. Probably bound and gagged and in the bottom of the car.

He pulled to a stop, his radiator abreast the left rear wheels. He leaped to the ground, right hand over the side of his machine.

"Want any help?" he asked blandly.

One of the two at the left rear wheel straightened up and his hand went to his pocket.

"Naw. Drive on, you so and so," he growled.

The jack leaped off the seat, and crashed on top of the

head of the surly one. The other man sprang at him, the jack smashed into his face.

The pair in the rear seat stood up, a revolver was brandished. Steve, the college high-jumper, soared quickly over the back of the touring car, as the weapon spoke three times.

But a man can't shoot straight if a human catapult is driving at him. All three bullets went wide and Steve Cobb's left hand grasped the gunman by the throat while his right gripped the throat of the fourth bandit who was frozen, apparently. The entire affair had taken hardly a couple of seconds, and this fellow was slow-witted. With a horrid crack of bone, the two heads were driven together, and the two unconscious men were thrown out of the car and landed heavily in the ditch.

In the bottom of the tonneau, lay Lucinda. She was drugged and unconscious. She had a man's overcoat over her night dress, her tiny bare feet protruding beyond its hem. Her hair was down and flowing. Her hat had fallen off.

Above her had been performed a prodigious feat of strength and valor and she was unaware of it. She was unaware of Steve Cobb gazing down upon her yearningly, his face working convulsively. Suddenly there was a sound of an automobile horn beside him.

Steve whirled, picking off the back seat a revolver which had dropped there from the inert hand of one of the bandits. The third car had stopped and two uniformed policemen had alighted and were hurrying forward.

"What's going on here?" demanded one of them. "Good God, wholesale murder!"

He stared at the still and bleeding forms behind the kidnapers' car.

"Kidnapers," said Steve, who leaped over the side of the car. "And there's the victim. Miss Lucinda Warburton of Cobbport. She's drugged, I guess."

"Say!" cried the second cop. "You mean to say you knocked out these four men? Lemme see this girl." He peered over the side of the car. "By gum, it's a girl and she's doped all right. Say mister, I take off my hat to you."

THE SECOND OFFICER had been inspecting the victims of the car jack. "One of 'em's dead," he said, rising from his knees. "Small loss, I guess." He produced a little red book and a pencil.

"What's your name, mister?" he demanded. "How come you knew about this?"

Steve hesitated and the officer's eye fell casually upon the roadster drawn up in the middle of the road which was brightly illuminated by the headlights from the police car. His eyes grew sharp as he read the number.

"Say," he cried. "This is the car stolen a couple of hours ago at Hyannis. Same license number. Packard roadster. And the chauffeur's description was a guy about eight feet tall."

Steve whipped the revolver of the bandit from the pocket of his trousers.

"Stick 'em up, both of you," he cried harshly. "Quick." Both policemen were within range. Their hands went up and their jaws dropped. Steve disarmed them in a trice.

"Get into your bus and get going," he said savagely. "You're too smart for your own good. Lift the young lady out and take her with you."

Meekly the policemen obeyed. Had they wished to make a fight of it the spectacle of the four dead or unconscious kidnapers would have deterred them. They placed Lucinda tenderly in the police car, got in and started toward Plymouth. For the moment their teeth had been drawn.

Steve climbed back into the stolen roadster, glanced at the gas gauge and saw that the tank was almost empty. He ran it down a sideroad a hundred feet ahead and then into a field.

After that he returned, rolled the victims of his hands and the auto jack into the ditch, finished the work on the tire, took possession of the touring car and started back down the Cape.

Within a couple of hours the entire police force of Eastern Massachusetts would be on his trail and, well as he knew the environs of Cobbport, he couldn't hide out long. His person was unusual—his description would be recognized everywhere.

That didn't bother him much. He had to attend to the matter of the green yawl. With his bonds once more in his possession, he would gladly surrender and take his chances at the hands of a Massachusetts jury instead of submitting to the tender mercies of Warburton and Clews.

In the meantime he had thirty or forty miles to travel before he reached Cobbport and there was an excellent chance of trouble en route. He observed that there was plenty of gas in the touring car and he hit her up to seventy within a couple of minutes.

Anyway, Lucinda was safe. If he hadn't been crazy he would never have dared to tackle four armed men. And it was crazy luck that he had achieved the rescue. The police car would start back as soon as the police secured weapons and turned Lucinda over to a physician. He wondered if she would recognize from his description as her rescuer the hulking brute she had called him at their previous meeting. He grinned. It was sort of too bad she hadn't seen the fight. Such a fight would not happen soon again.

Those cops in back would shoot to kill if they ever caught up with him so he had better not let them catch up with him.

He roared into the village. Ahead he saw an automobile being turned sidewise in the road. So they had phoned from the first house. There were two officers in the car. They honked warningly. Steve honked back and increased his speed. The police car held its post until the last minute and, seeing that the fugitive would not stop, had stepped on the gas. The car went tearing into a field, dipped into a ditch and overturned, as he observed when he flashed by. More trouble at the next town. Well, it was certainly an exciting night.

Weirdly enough, Steve Cobb, the convert to the doctrine of *dolce far niente,* the young man who for weeks had led the life of a lizard on land and a fish in the sea, was neither frightened nor distressed by his predicament. Every man's hand was against him and he was enjoying himself.

The car thundered over the Cape Cod Canal roadway, eating up the miles. At Buzzard's Bay, a big settlement, the police would be on the watch out for him, but he'd get through.

Next on the docket was an interview with a man named Clews.

19

THE NEW YORK BOAT

THOSE FUNNY CAPE Cod cops sticking a car across the road. And the pair who doubtless were in pursuit, their hearts in their mouth. He laughed wildly and then his laugh broke off and he gasped with dismay. From an eminence in the road he could see the Buzzard's Bay entrance to the Cape Cod Canal and the drawbridge was rising.

An insurmountable obstacle. A wall of steel, fifty or sixty feet high blocking the road, making it impassable, even for a superman with two hundred pounds of bone and muscle and a motor car with a hundred twenty synthetic horses under its hood.

Checkmate! Police coming down from Plymouth. Police no doubt closing in from Taunton and coming up the Cape. Should he surrender? Months in jail waiting for trial. A getting together of Warburton and Clews. That he owned the bonds was something they couldn't get over but—if they destroyed them and doctored the Cobb company records, how could he prove that they contained a clause preventing re-financing?

He had slowed his approach—no longer need of haste and the car ran upon another little hilltop. And, out in the

Bay, moving slowly and majestically toward the shore was a great steamer—the New York Boston night boat.

So it wasn't a police trap. This was the hour when the boat from New York entered the Canal from Buzzard's Bay.

Steve Cobb proceeded another quarter of a mile, stopped the car and abandoned it. He sped across lots toward the bridge. Even at this hour there were a few cars waiting and a score or so of persons watching. The passage from Boston to New York of the great steamers through the Canal will never cease to be exciting to Cape Cod folks and even in the small hours of the morning some of them turn out for the event.

At eight P.M. when the steamer from Boston proceeds through the Canal she is accompanied by scores of motor cars on the road which runs parallel to the waterway while hundreds of interested spectators line the bridges.

Steve reached the edge of the canal, slipped under the bridge and went rapidly out toward the draw upon the supporting girders. He arrived after several moments at the edge of the draw just as the sharp prow of the big ship entered. She was so broad of beam that there were only four or five feet between her rail and side of the draw. Steve stood perched on a broad steel beam level with the lower deck. The vessel was moving very slowly, no more than five or six miles an hour. Her passengers were either asleep or grouped on the top deck. Her crew were at their stations and the bulk of the vessel concealed the fugitive from view of persons on the State Bridge. If he leaped and missed and dropped into the water he would be ground to jelly between ship and bridge foundations but he didn't take that into consideration. He hurled himself forward, grasped the rail with powerful hands, withstood the shock of contact between his stomach and the steel side of the ship, pulled himself over and dropped flat.

He lay on the deck for five minutes, then rose and looked back. The drawbridge was being lowered and the ship was moving a little faster. There was nobody in sight. On the other hand there were bright lights all along the shore of the canal and if he went overboard he would be seen. Also, in this narrow waterlane, his prospects of avoiding the screws of the steamer would be slight.

It looked as though he was bound for Boston. Of course he could insert his advertisements in the newspapers there, but, knowing in whose hands the bonds were, it was certain that Warburton would get them and they would vanish off the face of the earth. Besides, he'd be tagged as a stowaway by the time the ship reached her pier and his description would be in all the morning papers as a man wanted for murder and other crimes. He had to get off the ship somehow.

During the hour it took for the passage through the Canal, Steve squatted in a corner of that unfrequented deck and had plenty of time to consider how many kinds of fool he had been.

In the first place, he should have left the bonds in his New York safety deposit box. If he had brought them to the Cape, he should have placed them in a bank there. But he had no expectation that Warburton would come to Cobbport or that he dared take illegal methods to secure the bond issue. It had rather amused him to put them in a shoe box and tuck them on a rafter of the hut in which he lived while Warburton shivered and shook in his New York offices wondering when the overlooked securities would turn up to menace him.

HE HAD TO admit that he had gone a long way towards General Burton's outlook on life. Nothing seemed to matter, not even his punishment of the man who had defrauded his father. He had not really suspected foul play in connection with the death of Ezra Cobb. It was curious that a strong healthy man should sicken and die in so short a time, but, like most people, Steve was incredulous that business enemies would resort to murder.

Knowing that Warburton had sent Hutton after the bonds, he had been insane to leave them behind him when he towed the remains of Hutton out to sea. In fact, looking back over the past few days, it was obvious to Steve Cobb that he had behaved throughout as an imbecile. And it was by no means certain that he wouldn't have to pay the penalty for murder when he had only exercised the rights of a householder to defend himself.

Well, before he met a disgraceful fate, he would put a finish to the plot of Clews and Mrs. Warburton and send Warburton's financial structure toppling like a house of cards.

After a while Steve dozed. Since early evening he had been through enough to weary a dozen men and his six mile swim was only a part of it. He awakened when the ship gave a slight roll. In a flash Steve was up and looking over the rail. She was out of the Canal and just outside the Sandwich breakwater. She was still moving slowly.

Instantly Steve was upon the rail. He hurled himself headlong into the water, landing twenty-five feet from the side of the ship, diving deep and swimming fast. As he had boarded the steamer only a hundred feet from her bow he escaped the suction of the screws and struck out for the shore.

Twenty minutes later, in an old Ford which its owner had trustingly left unlocked in the driveway of his house in Sandwich, Steve was rolling down the Cape Cod Bay road at thirty miles an hour, all the machine could possibly manage. He had to change a tire ten miles along, but he encountered no one either on the main road or the cutoff to the Sound shore.

When he drove in to Cobbport, dawn was breaking.

The sunrise was indescribably lovely, but Steve had seen many Cape sunrises. He left the car in the main street, rushed down to the shore and gazed across the harbor.

The green yawl was gone.

Steve sank down upon the beach, sick at heart and swept by despair. That Clews had men on board who had given evidence of their willingness to fight for their employer had not deterred him in his purpose in the least. He hadn't considered them. He had returned to Cobbport determined to board the yawl and recover his property despite hell and high water and he had not given the slightest consideration to possible failure.

Evidently Clews had put into the Haven just long enough to send Diana ashore and had immediately departed. He had likely slipped into some other port— but which? There were many yacht harbors along this coast and he might have selected any one of them.

Meanwhile the sun was coming up and very shortly the fishermen would be coming down to the beach. He had to hide. Wearily he rose and plodded toward the General's cottage. He'd write the ads, give them to Burton, return his money and decide what steps he would take to keep out of the hands of the police until he had accomplished his purpose.

Clews would be sure to return to confer with his woman partner.

The General was asleep in his bed but woke as the door opened.

"That you Steve?" he quavered.

"It's me all right," replied the youth dispiritedly.

"Did you bring her back? Was she hurt any?" asked the old fellow thrusting a pair of naked and incredibly skinny legs upon the floor.

"She's all right," said Steve. "I caught them halfway to Plymouth. I turned her over to the police."

"I bet she was grateful to you," cried the old man. "Just like out of a story book; you riding to the rescue. How did you catch 'em, Steve? Last I seen of you you was running the other way."

"I picked up a car and chased them."

"How come the police didn't arrest you on account of that Hutton business?"

"I didn't hang round. Lucinda was drugged. She doesn't know how she escaped. General, I took your wallet. Here it is. I'm going to write some advertisements. I want you to loan me about thirty dollars to pay for them. Will you put them in the post as soon as the post office opens?"

"Thirty dollars. That's a powerful lot of money," whined the ancient. "Won't have much left."

"I'll pay you back."

He nodded. "I guess it's all right. I went up to Warburton's and woke 'em up. Mr. Warburton he was terrible excited, but I told him you was sure to catch 'em, the dirty kidnapers. Mrs. Warburton, she was excited, too.

"He notified the police for miles around and then got out his car and went after 'em. I got awful tired a couple of hours ago and come to bed."

"Had Warburton returned when you left?"

"Guess not. Probably he's back now, though."

For ten minutes Steve was busy writing at the decrepit table upon scraps of paper found in the General's top bureau drawer.

"Here's the notices," he said. "Get envelopes and stamps and put these newspaper addresses on them. I've got to be going."

"Where you goin' Steve?"

Steve grinned. "You'd be surprised," he replied. "I'll be calling on you soon."

20

TWO HEROES ARE REWARDED

LUCINDA WARBURTON AWOKE in a strange bed in a hotel in Plymouth. There was a nurse in starched white sitting by her bedside. The sun was pouring in through two large windows which were open so she could hear the roar of the surf piling up on the beach without.

The nurse was bending over her instantly.

"How do you feel, Miss Warburton?" she asked anxiously.

Lucinda smiled up at her. "Not bad. I have a slight headache and I'm hungry." She shuddered. "How did I get here? Where is this place? Where are those horrible men?"

"They're gone. Everything is fine. You're in the Pilgrim Hotel. Your father is downstairs waiting to see you."

"I thought maybe it had been a nightmare. Was I actually carried off?"

"You owe your rescue to two splendid police officers," said the nurse. "The whole story is in the morning papers."

"They pulled me out of my bed and took me into a car and I knew I was being kidnapped," said Lucinda sitting up and much excited. "As we left the estate I saw General Burton and Steve Cobb. I yelled at them and the men choked me and then they gave me chloroform. I suppose it was chloroform."

"You were unconscious when the officers found you," explained the nurse. "There was a terrific battle, two of the criminals are dead and two are badly wounded. One of them escaped. He's a murderer. The whole police force of the State are in pursuit of him. Imagine two policemen attacking five desperate criminals."

"I kind of hoped that Steve Cobb would rescue me," said Lucinda plaintively. "He's so big and strong—"

"Steve Cobb! Did you say Steve Cobb?"

"Yes."

"But he's the murderer. The head kidnapper."

"You must be crazy," said Lucinda. "Steve wouldn't kidnap me. He doesn't like me enough." She grinned wryly. "And how can he be a murderer? Steve wouldn't kill anybody. Besides, I saw him on the road with the General."

"I don't know anything about this General, but most likely he was the 'lookout'," said the nurse knowingly. "Criminals always have a 'lookout.' He joined them after they chloroformed you."

"I'd like to see my father," said Lucinda. "You don't know what you're talking about."

"I'll go fetch him," replied the nurse crossly. "I guess you must be delirious."

There was an interesting scene taking place in the sitting room of the suite taken by William Warburton on the floor below. The Mayor of Plymouth was there and the manager of the hotel and the local chief of police and officers Nutley and Brown of Plymouth County.

Officers Nutley and Brown were the pair who had taken Lucinda to Plymouth after being disarmed by Steve Cobb. They were a couple of shrewd Yankees who had been deeply humiliated by their treatment and in no mood to blazon to the world a true narrative of their experience.

They knew that they would be dismissed from the force if they confessed that they had been put to flight by a single crook, but, as officer Nutley pointed out as they drove along with the unconscious Lucinda between them, there were no witnesses of their disgrace.

"Nobody's going to believe that thief," said Nutley. Here's a kidnapped girl and if she wasn't awful rich, she wouldn't have been kidnapped. Them yeggs back there don't know what struck them, judging by the way they got bowled over. What's to stop us from claiming we did it?"

"This big fellow."

"We take the girl to a doctor and go back and straighten things up there. Take the wounded kidnappers in as prisoners. We cleaned them up, see. This car thief came along and beat it when we recognized the stolen car. We couldn't chase him because we got the girl to think about."

"When he's pinched he'll tell a different yarn."

"It's two against one. What have we got to lose?"

THEY PICKED UP a doctor a few miles along the road who accompanied them into Plymouth. They returned immediately to the scene of the battle and to their delight found their weapons where Steve had dropped them in the ditch alongside of the dead and injured kidnappers. Thus fortified they went back to Plymouth, told their tale and were now reaping the benefit. An alarm had gone out for the fleeing car thief, as a result of a phone call from the doctor's residence and the description given was recognized by the wounded State officer Noonan at Cobbport as the murder suspect and fugitive Steve Cobb. That Cobb was wanted for murder gave the cops assurance in their version of the affair.

"You may admit the newspaper men," said William Warburton as he rose from his chair. Immediately the door was opened and there filed in three reporters and two camera men.

"Take seats, gentleman," said Mr. Warburton in an urbane manner. He had returned to his residence after two hours of aimless driving about Cape Cod roads to be informed that Lucinda was safe in Plymouth after a heroic rescue. He had packed a bag and started immediately north. He was arrayed in sharply creased English flannel trousers, and a natty blue coat. He was freshly shaved, and his ruddy color and mustache gave him the appearance of a benevolent aristocrat, a master of men and money and he was about to do something most unusual in the type he represented, something requiring an audience, reporters and cameras. He was going to give away money.

"Gentlemen," he said, "a dreadful outrage has been committed. My only daughter was torn from her home in Cobbport by dastardly criminals, drugged, and an attempt made to take her to some criminal hangout in Boston. In these days of lawlessness and unrest, of banditry and brigandage, the only protection to honest people is the police. At times it seems as if the police are an inadequate instrument of defense.

"It gives me all the more pleasure to testify that upon this occasion they have been magnificently efficient.

"The kidnappers were pursued by officers Nutley and Brown, two young men following a dangerous profession with stout hearts. They overtook five armed bandits and unhesitatingly attacked them. When their guns were empty they fought on with a motor jack and their fists. They killed two of the criminals, severely injured two others and only one escaped.

"Thanks to them my beloved daughter is safe upstairs, sleeping like a child." His voice trembled. "I shudder to think of what her fate might have been. How many kidnapped persons have been slain by the miscreants into whose hands they have fallen. My gratitude to these brave policemen is beyond expression.

"Words are inadequate. And words cannot repay these men for what they have done for me. I have here two checks for one thousand dollars each. They are yours, Messrs. Nutley and Brown. Thank you and God bless you."

He handed the checks to the delighted officers and sat down, his feelings overcoming him. There was a clapping of hands. The fortunate policemen pocketed their money and departed. From their standpoint, so far so good.

One of the reporters rose.

"I'm Hammond of the Boston *Herald*, Mr. Warburton," he said. "There are features of this affair which puzzle me. May I ask you a few questions?"

"Certainly, young man," said Warburton benignly.

"There were five kidnappers," he said, "but one of them was traveling in a stolen Packard roadster, the others were in a touring car."

THE OFFICERS EXPLAINED that. "This man was accompanying them in an extra car in case of accidents. When the touring car had a blow-out, he drove up alongside to help them change their tire."

"I understand that. He fled down the Cape and escaped

"My bonds, damn you,"
growled Steve.

somehow. But State officer Noonan says that the description given of him answers to that of Stephen Cobb accused of murder in Cobbport."

"So I'm informed."

"I went to school with Steve Cobb, Mr. Warburton. I can't see him either as a kidnapper or murderer."

"Frankly," replied Warburton. "I'm astonished myself."

"He is the son of Ezra Cobb who formerly owned the Cobb Concrete Company which you now control."

"I don't see the point of your questions, young man."

"From what I gather, this man, Hutton, he is accused of killing worked for you."

"That's true," said Warburton whose urbanity rapidly was evaporating.

"What was the message he was taking from you to Steve Cobb, sir?"

The mayor rose. "Really, Mr. Warburton, I must apologize for this questionnaire. I hope you don't think I knew when I requested that reporters be admitted—"

But Warburton was in control of himself.

"I have no objection to answering that question. I sent Hutton to offer Mr. Cobb the post of sales-manager of the reorganized Cobb company."

"Say," cried Hammond excitedly. "Then you respected Steve. You wanted to give him his old job back."

"Right."

"I'm hanged if I see any reason for his killing a fellow who brought him good news."

"Nor do I," said Warburton dryly. "I think the charge is absurd. I don't know how Hutton met his death, but I feel confident that it was not at the hands of the son of my old friend Ezra Cobb."

Hammond gazed triumphantly at the other reporters. "Now ain't that something?" he demanded. "Say, Mr. Warburton, you're okay. Much obliged."

After necessary amenities with the other visitors, Warburton was left alone and wiped away sweat which had broken out on his brow. He was much mystified at the apparent connection of Steve Cobb with the kidnapping since.

21

WARBURTON GETS A SHOCK

IT WAS THE first time in Warburton's career he had to call in a murder monger—Hutton had always done his dirty work—and the kick back had been frightful. Fifty thousand dollars would have gone into criminal hands for the theft of the bonds and the assassination of Steve Cobb, and failing in their job they had intended to make him pay fifty thousand for the release of his daughter, perhaps twice that much. And he would have paid.

It was to his interest to have Steve Cobb at large rather than in police hands which explained why he had answered the reporter's questions. But Cobb at large was a menace. Cobb dead before Warburton had the bonds in his hands was unthinkable—as part of an estate, they would be tied up for months and Warburton and Company couldn't stand a delay of months.

The nurse entered. "Miss Warburton is awake and wants to see you," she stated.

"Coming."

He followed her upstairs. Lucinda, blooming like a rose and smiling, lay on the bed half sitting up against her pillows.

"Father," she explained. "I'm so glad you're here. Were you horribly worried?"

"I almost expired of anxiety," he replied, taking both her hands and gazing fondly down upon her. Warburton loved his daughter as much as he could anybody except himself and he was tremendously proud of her because she was beautiful.

"The nurse told me the most preposterous thing," she declared. "She said Steve Cobb was identified as one of the kidnappers."

"That's what the police say."

"It's absurd. I saw them. There were four men. We passed General Burton and Steve Cobb as the car turned into the beach road and I shouted for help. I saw the General first—Steve was in the shadow and before I could call to him, they covered my mouth."

"A man answering Cobb's description accompanied them in another car," he informed her, "that is according to the police. He took to flight when the officers attacked his companions."

"Why do you hate him?" she demanded with a curious sparkle in her eyes.

"My dear child, he hates me. He harbors rancor because I beat his father in a business battle. He broke into my house, made love to my wife—"

"I don't believe it," she said bluntly.

"He's not like that. I know."

"But you heard Diana say—"

"I don't believe a word she says about anything. Father— why do you put up with that woman? She doesn't love you—she treats you horribly—"

"Lucinda—there, there, dear, you are strained and nervous. Some other time we'll discuss Diana. I've made friendly overtures to this cub and I've been insulted for my pains."

"Either it wasn't Steve Cobb in the other car or if it was, he was trying to rescue me," she said firmly. "They have no right to accuse him of being a kidnapper. And what did the nurse mean by saying he is a murderer?"

"An attempt was made to arrest him for the murder of a man named Hutton, an—er—employee of mine and he was taken from the officers by outlaws, members of a gang he belongs to according to the State police."

"The Mr. Hutton who was at the house the other night? Is he dead?"

"His body was found at sea the next day, dear."

"Why are they persecuting Steve? He is the most harmless person—"

"He assaulted me in my own house, Lucinda," said her father sternly.

"But it was because you were going to shoot him, because you thought he and Diana—"

"We must cease this discussion. Are you able to return to Cobbport today?"

She nodded. "I'm all right. I can start any time. Father, I've a feeling I'd still be in those men's hands, if it had not been for Steve."

There was a flicker in Warburton's eyes. "Look here. Are you in love with this fellow?" he demanded.

"Certainly not!" she exclaimed angrily. "He's absolutely hateful but—but—if I were in trouble, he might be grand."

The nurse came into the room. "A phone call for you, sir, from Woods Hole. Will you take it here?"

He hesitated. "No, switch it to the apartment below. We'll start back in an hour or two, Lucinda, if you feel up to it."

"I'll be quite up to it," she replied.

Warburton went below and picked up the phone.

"Warburton speaking," he said. "Who is this, please?"

"John Clews, Mr. Warburton."

"Clews, eh? How did you know where I was and what do you want?" he demanded gruffly.

"Phoned your house and Mrs. Warburton said you were there. Regarding what I want, I have bonds to sell."

"Communicate with my office in New York. I'm vacationing on Cape Cod."

CLEWS CHUCKLED. "COBB COMPANY first issue, six per cents. Interested?" he asked softly.

Warburton gripped the back of the chair against which he was standing until the knuckles turned white. "You mean—"

"Precisely."

"Er— May I ask how they came into your possession?"

"As legitimately as your possession of the Cobb Company, Mr. Warburton."

"If you can show a clear title, I am interested."

"Have they caught this murderer Cobb, yet?" asked Clews with apparent inconsequence.

"I don't know."

"Let's hope they don't. I'm sailing into Cobbport this afternoon. Will you be at home at eleven this evening?"

"Yes. Care to state your price?"

"Half of everything you've got," said Clews and hung up the receiver upon a man who looked as though he were going to have apoplexy.

Warburton sank slowly to a chair.

Clews, the yachtsman, owner of the green yawl Emerald, which had been entering and leaving Cobbport for several days and apparently had no business there. Clews, the unscrupulous broker and promoter. How had Clews learned of the existence of the bonds. A leak in the Warburton office? Nobody but the auditor and himself knew the peculiar features of the bonds, not even his partners? The presence of Steve Cobb in the village had brought Clews there as it had brought Warburton.

Had Hutton secured the bonds from Cobb and had been waylaid and knocked on the head by Clews? That would explain why Cobb had broken into Warburton's house—he had missed his securities and assumed that Warburton had stolen them. It was a plausible theory.

Warburton clapped his hands together with a loud smack. Why, it explained the rescue of Cobb from the police. The men from the yawl. With Steve at large to prove ownership, Clews couldn't sell the bonds. Had he forced Cobb to make them over to him? Remembering the solidity of Steve's jaw, Warburton doubted that.

It was probable that Clews was bluffing. Cobb was a fugitive and, if he had made a deal with the broker, he would have remained in the yawl to avoid arrest. Instead Cobb was roaming the countryside, stealing cars, mixing up with kidnappers. If, in the small hours of this morning Cobb had been seen outside Plymouth, he certainly could not be on board the yawl at Woods Hole.

Warburton lighted a cigar and walked up and down the room. The game wasn't up. Clews, backed by Cobb, would hold out for millions and Warburton would have to pay. But if he could get the securities away from Clews, and one of these Cape Cod officers shot Steve Cobb, the house of Warburton and Company was stronger than ever before.

With all his speculations regarding the source of Clews' knowledge, it never occurred to William Warburton to suspect Diana. He knew that Clews was an acquaintance of hers but he was not aware that she had been visiting the yawl. He had been sound asleep when she slipped out in the night before and had been awakened half an hour later by the hundred year old General Burton who was insistently ringing the doorbell.

HE HAD TO get back to Cobbport as soon as possible. He phoned down stairs.

"Tell my chauffeur to bring the car round," he commanded, "and send up my bill."

If there was some way of reaching an agreement with Steve Cobb. He remembered the vehemence of Lucinda. She was interested in the fellow. Cobb must reciprocate if the child had any foundation to her theory that he was concerned in her rescue. Why not? The lad was decent and came of a fine family. Suddenly he blushed.

There came back to him the words of a dead man found floating on the surface of the Atlantic.

"You figured you had a couple of vamps to sic on him. Which do you use, your wife or your daughter?"

He ought to have shot the scoundrel dead in his tracks,

only he was very useful. He deserved what had happened to him the same night, the hound.

After a minute, Warburton phoned downstairs. "If they are still about, please send officers Nutley and Brown over here," he requested.

"The car is here, sir."

"Let it wait."

It was a very different sort of Warburton whom the heroic policemen encountered when they entered the scene of their recent triumph.

"I want no nonsense and no lies from you fellows," he said harshly. "A witness of the affair of the Cape Cod road has turned up."

The alarm and embarrassment of the officers was all Warburton needed to inform him that their report of the rescue of Lucinda was incomplete.

Officer Brown shot a glance of terror at Nutley. Nutley's face grew red and he shifted his weight from one foot to the other.

"You may keep those checks and what you tell me will be in confidence," said the financier. "But I want the truth. Speak out."

Brown looked beseechingly at Nutley. Nutley coughed loudly.

"We had to do it, sir," he pleaded, "or we'd have lost our jobs."

"Tell me exactly what happened and tell the truth."

"You won't let it go no farther, sir?"

"No."

"Well, the fact is, when we came up, this big feller had

knocked out all four of them. He hit them with the motor jack."

"That's what I thought. Go on."

"He told us who the lady was and asked us to take her to the doctor.

"Just then I noticed the Packard he was driving and it was one that had been stolen down near Hyannis. I asked him about it and he pulled a gun. Thinking he had rescued the girl, see, we didn't have our guns in our hands. Well, he took them away from us and made us drive on with the lady.

"When we come back after him we found our guns where he had thrown them and Joe and me, we decided, seeing he was a crook—"

"To pose as a couple of heroes," Warburton sneered. "Get the hell out of here."

He went upstairs to Lucinda.

"Child," he said, "I've just got the truth out of those policemen. Your friend Steve stole a car, gave chase to the kidnappers, attacked them single handed—"

"Oh, father," cried Lucinda. She flung herself at him, kissed him violently and burst into tears. He stroked her hair.

"He's a most remarkable young man," he said. "I agree with you that the murder charge is absurd. In fact I have a notion who did kill Hutton. I have no objection whatever to your friendship with Steve Cobb when his reputation is cleared up."

"You are the most adorable father in the world," she exclaimed.

Warburton had the grace to color.

"Ready to go now?"

"Uh, huh," she said, wiping her eyes. Her face lengthened. "Trouble is he is very nasty to me. He's perfectly rotten." Suddenly she smiled. "Just the same, if he chased those criminals forty miles and fought four of them on account of me, probably he thinks I'm pretty nice at that."

"Of course he does," said Warburton.

22

UNDER THE EAVES

STEVE COBB WOKE up in a bed about the time Lucinda Warburton was awaking from her drugged sleep in Plymouth. He had slept so heavily that it was hard to resume the business of being awake. Sunlight was pouring through a small circular window and for a moment he thought it was a porthole and he was back on Clews' yawl, a prisoner.

During the past forty-eight hours his physical exertions had been tremendous and he had had almost no rest. By the brightness of the sun, he judged it to be mid-morning. He stretched luxuriously, yawned and sat up. He grinned as everything came back and he recognized his bed chamber. He was in the topmost attic of the Ezra Cobb residence, now the home of William Warburton. In this attic, rubbish had been accumulating for thirty or forty years.

The place was half filled with old trunks, with boxes, and broken furniture. He was laying in a four poster bed but one of the posts had been broken off. The mattress was made of straw and there was no bedding but Steve had covered himself with an extremely dusty rug he had pulled off the floor. There were cobwebs across the window pane. There were cobwebs on the walls and ceiling, and there was a musty aroma. He sneezed and dust came out of his nostrils.

The events of the night came crowding back, the battle in his hut, the incidents on the yawl, the six mile swim, the theft of the car, the kidnapping of Lucinda, the terrific fight on the Plymouth road, the leap to the New York boat, his departure from it and his arrival in Cobbport.

"No wonder I was tired," said Steve aloud. He wasn't afraid to speak out. This attic was under the eaves of the huge house—it was a storeroom, probably not yet discovered by the Warburtons, and nobody was in the least likely to visit it.

As a child, Steve had played in this funny old attic. There were all sorts of interesting things in the trunks; junk, of course, but interesting to an inquiring boy.

He got up and peered out of the high circular window from which there was a view of the port. The yawl hadn't returned.

By this time the whole state of Massachusetts was looking for Steve Cobb, but about the last place in which the police would look would be the home of William Warburton.

He had secured admission to the house shortly after sunrise by the same kitchen window through which he had entered before and he had made his way immediately to Mrs. Warburton's chamber. Diana would know where the yawl had gone and if and when it was coming back. But the room was empty and the mistress of the house had gone. He knew she had returned just before the kidnapping of Lucinda and she must have sailed away on the yawl within an hour or two. It looked as if she had finally departed from the bed and board of William Warburton.

Her bed had been turned down and rumpled as though she had lain in it for a brief period and Steve had an almost irresistible urge to lay down upon it and rest. He was about finished physically. Half an hour or an hour's rest would do so much for him. He moved toward it and had strength to stop. If he closed his eyes he probably wouldn't open them for many hours and then he would find himself in the hands of the enemy. But he must sleep. He couldn't go on.

And suddenly he remembered the attic, remembered there was a broken down bed up there. It was most unlikely anybody would go up there and it would never occur to search Warburton's house for the man accused of killing Warburton's friend.

There was no lock on the door of the attic, but he lifted a heavy trunk and pushed it against the inside of the door and he had had a delicious sleep, five or six hours at least. Unfortunately there was no running water in the place and he couldn't wash. Stripping he gave himself a dry rub and massaged himself as well as he could and felt refreshed. He was, however, ravenously hungry. Nothing could be done about that. It would be madness to show himself. And he had to hide in this place until night.

He went back and lay down on the bed. His reflections were bitter. The predicament in which he found himself was the result of having parked his brains and indulged his muscles since his arriving at Cape Cod. Having in his possession property of great value, he had been too indolent to put it in a place of safety.

On the other hand, if the bonds had been locked in a

vault, his own life would still have been in danger. Steve had no close relatives. If he died the bonds would go to distant cousins who would have gladly sold them to Warburton for what would seem a reasonable offer.

HE HADN'T THOUGHT much about the manner in which he would use them against the despoiler of his father—in fact the philosophy of General Burton had so numbed him that he didn't think about them at all. Warburton's anxiety to eliminate their menace had stirred things up. It had amused Steve to refuse the man's offers to purchase—he expected to have a lot of fun watching the fellow wriggle and stew.

If only he had called in Chief Eben Cobb, told the truth about the death of Hutton and put the bonds in the bank next morning—well, there was no sense in worrying about his mistakes. Tonight he'd take the field again. Maybe the yawl would return. He wondered how Lucinda was. Probably all right and more beautiful than ever—funny how that kid had got under his skin, made him forget everything except her peril. Had the kidnappers been taken to a hospital?—of course they had—if he had killed them all, death would have been too good for them. How had the chauffeur and his girl friend come out. He hoped the poor devils wouldn't lose their jobs.

Steve was asleep again, sleeping more heavily than ever. Many hours passed and he slept on. He didn't hear the turning of the doorknob, nor the effort to push open the door. He didn't even hear the trunk slithering across the floor. When he slept, he slept.

What woke him was a warm moist softness against his lips. He opened his eyes and looked into a pair of amazingly beautiful dark ones. There was a flushed lovely face close to his and a weight on his chest.

Steve sat up so suddenly and violently that Diana Warburton was flung backwards. Their foreheads had come into collision and one of her hands covered her left temple.

"You brute!" she exclaimed. Then she smiled. "You adorable brute!"

Steve looked about wildly. She was alone. The trunk had been pushed away but the door had been closed. He grinned wickedly.

"Taking advantage of me, eh?"

"Such a surprise, sweetheart," she murmured. She wore a house dress of black with yellow trimming.

After all, he thought, he had come to this house to find this woman and squeeze information from her. Daylight had imprisoned him in this attic and fate had sent her to him since he couldn't go in search of her.

"Listen, you beautiful thief in the night," he said grimly, "cut out the sentiment. You're as cold blooded as a fish and as unscrupulous as a hyena. How did you happen to come up to this attic?"

She smiled. "I love attics. I've been intending to explore this one for days."

"Where were you last night?" he demanded. "Where's the yawl?"

"My dear boy, I'm so glad to see you. I almost died when you jumped overboard. I didn't believe anybody could reach the shore. Why did you treat us like that, Steve? We're your friends. Your only friends."

"Yes? Have you heard from Lucinda?"

She shrugged her shoulders. "Oh, the brat's all right.

She's in her room below. She's babbling about your heroism."

"She is? How did she know I—"

"No other human being could possibly have attacked four armed men and smashed them to pieces. I positively adore you, Steve. I worship you."

"Yeh. Suppose you hand over my bonds."

"Your bonds?" she asked as though astonished.

"Stow that. You and Clews stole my bonds. They were no good to you without me, so you kidnapped me from the police. After Clews had me knocked on the head and thrown overboard, he would get together with your murderer of a husband and do business."

"STEVE," SHE CRIED. "You're mad! Why all we wanted was to have you work with us. Why, I love you."

"Pshaw, you love Clews and your husband, for all I know. You're a thoroughly selfish and wicked woman and I've had enough of your nonsense. Give me my bonds."

"I haven't got them," she said sullenly.

"Then Clews has them."

She didn't answer.

"Where's the yawl?"

"I left it this morning in Woods Hole."

"Humph. You're not home much."

"As little as possible," she said shortly.

He eyed her malevolently.

"Why don't you beat me?" she demanded. "I'd love it."

Steve rose from the bed and walked to the door and pushed the trunk in position against it.

"All I have to do is to scream," she stated coolly.

"You're playing with Clews against your husband," he

replied. "So you don't want me to fall into Warburton's hands and you don't want the police to get me. Go ahead and scream."

She placed her hands behind her head, pushed herself over on the bed and leaned back against the wall. She smiled at him bewitchingly.

"I love being up here alone with you," she said ardently. "Why should I rouse the household?"

"You beat the world!" he cried, perplexed and not unmoved.

She stretched our her arms.

"Obey that impulse. Come over here and kiss me, beloved."

"I'm much more likely to choke you," he said angrily. "Now you listen, Diana. Your husband is responsible for my father's death. I'll make no truce with him. If I ever saw scoundrel, Jack Clews is one. I'll do no business with him. And, knowing you as I do, you couldn't vamp me if you were ten times as attractive."

Diana pursed her lips suggestively. Steve turned away his head. The hot blood coursed through his veins. A man may hate and despise a woman but acknowledge her physical charm.

"You remind me of a fox telling the hounds where they get off," she said sardonically. "Don't forget, my friend, that you killed a man and are wanted by the police. We have your bonds. Without them you can't injure my husband. You haven't money enough to hire a lawyer. The bonds are negotiable. I doubt if you could prove ownership. Anyway, if Warburton buys them from us, retires them as of six months back, and produced evidence that you sold them to him at that time, the word of a condemned murderer won't be believed against that of William Warburton. You're on a spot."

STEVE GAZED AT her sullenly. He recognized the logic of what she said. Unfortunately Mrs. Warburton didn't know when to stop talking.

"Steve," she said. "You're young and magnificent but you're a bit stupid. Clews is an old acquaintance and you remember the other night on the yawl—there's no sentimental relationship between us. I owe him nothing. I learned about the bonds. I made Clews accompany me to your house that night and I sent him to rescue you from the gangsters Warburton imported to take you to New York where you could be tortured into doing business with him. He went in because he saw money for himself. We don't need him. Suppose you and I form a partnership. We'll leave here tonight, phone Warburton that we are together and make him pay us a million, maybe more, for the bonds."

Steve's smile was bland. He walked to the window, took down the long knotted rope which hung on a nail beside it and to serve as a fire escape.

"What on earth are you doing?" she demanded. "Listen to me."

STEVE POUNCED UPON her. One big hand covered her mouth and pressed her down on the bed. He pulled the handkerchief from her belt, pried open her lower jaw and thrust the handkerchief into the mouth. While her eyes hurled darts of hate, he ripped away the hem of her dress and made use of it to gag her after which he bound her securely with the rope. When she was unable to move hand or foot he looked down on her contemptuously.

"So you're in a position to double cross Clews as well as Warburton," he observed. "That means that you have the bonds. And I've a hunch that you've hidden them in this attic. That's what brought you up here."

During the next two hours Cobb worked methodically while the wretched woman followed his progress with her eyes.

Searching the place was a prodigious job. There were at least a dozen trunks full of every sort of rubbish, including many articles that brought to Steve memories of his childhood. There were half a dozen big boxes, innumerable small packages and bundles. When he had gone through all of these, he sought for loose boards in the floor and found none. Finally he lifted the squirming Diana off the bed and laid her on the floor after which he tore the old mattress apart. Not a nook or cranny of the attic he knew so well missed inspection. Finally, with a sigh, he abandoned the search. He had been wrong. The bonds were not there.

She wore a thin dress with little chance of concealing a bulky object and he passed his hands over her and decided they were not on her person. By her wrist-watch he saw it was five in the afternoon. If not in the attic they must be hidden in her chamber.

He had to go down to the second floor walk the length of the house and if he escaped the eyes of a servant, risk being caught for the second time in his wife's room by Warburton.

"I'm going down to rip your pretty bedroom apart, Diana. I don't suppose you wish me luck," he said.

She made inarticulate sounds denoting rage and her eyes flamed. Steve laid her on the torn mattress, pulled away the trunk, opened the door and stepped out. There was a narrow hall and staircase. He descended cautiously and reached the second floor. The hall was empty and he went along to the main corridor which also was empty. Without encountering anybody he reached Mrs. Warburton's room, pushed open the door and entered.

23

LUCK TURNS

THERE WERE DAINTY feminine touches about a room which had been furnished for a man in the heavy fashion of a past generation. There were no hiding places, secret panels, wall safes and such devices—the bonds would be in drawers of the dresser, the bureau, in boxes or bags or hidden in the mattress.

Steve's methods were those of a man in haste and who had no regard for the feelings of the owner of the establishment. He pulled suitcases and hat boxes out of the closets and dumped their contents on the floor. He took down and inspected each gown and dropped it on the floor of the closet. He pulled out every drawer, overturned it, thrust his hands through the disordered piles of lingerie and toilet accessories. He removed the mattress from the bed and inspected it for sewn up slits.

When he was finished, the room presented an appearance which beggars description. With a sigh of disappointment he stood in the middle of the room and surveyed the havoc which he had created. Nothing doing.

He glanced out through the window and stiffened. The green yawl Emerald was in and picking up her moorings.

His eye wandered and saw on the top shelf of one of

the closets a paper box which had been invisible from the closet itself. With a mutter of excitement he rushed into the closet and pulled down the box. It contained a pair of dance slippers done up in tissue paper. And it was then the door opened.

"Mrs. Warburton," said a woman's voice, "I want to talk to you."

Lucinda. He heard Lucinda exclaim at the appearance of the room and he emerged from the closet.

"Steve Cobb," the girl cried shrilly. "What is the meaning of this?"

"You'll find your stepmother in the attic, Lucinda," said Steve with a mad laugh. "All bound round with a woolen string."

He rushed to the window and pushed up the screen.

"Steve," cried Lucinda. "I don't understand. Steve, I want to tell you—"

"I have to see a man," Steve tossed over his shoulder as he went through the window, ran down the sloping porch roof, hung by his hands and dropped upon the lawn. Lucinda was leaning out the window, speechless with astonishment and bewilderment and she saw a streak of white tearing towards the water's edge.

Steve was in the water. He yanked off his sneakers, unloosened his belt and slipped out of the duck pants. He pulled off the sweater and wearing only the trunks in which he had come ashore the previous night, struck out for the yacht.

While it may appear at times as if Steve Cobb acted as rationally as an infuriated bull, his determination to board the yawl was not entirely unreasonable.

He was forced out of his refuge by the appearance of Lucinda. Lucinda had caught him, apparently, robbing her mother's room. She would summon her father, call the servants, make a search for her stepmother and perhaps summon the police.

Outside the house he was in territory where everybody knew him and knew he was wanted by the officers. On board the yawl was Clews with the stolen bonds in his possession and this was probably the only chance left to recover his property. Since Diana didn't have the bonds, Clews must have them.

He didn't fear the crew of the yawl. If he could slip on board, he'd rush those fellows and smack them right and left before they recovered from their surprise. Daylight hampered his chances but he never bothered much about chances. All he regretted as he slid swiftly through the sea was that he had discarded his pants before removing the kidnapper's revolver which was in the right hand pocket. However, immersion in water for five or ten minutes was apt to make it useless.

The crew of the yawl had made fast to the mooring as he approached and apparently paid no attention to the head of a swimmer approaching from the direction of Warburton's. Steve approached the yawl at the stern, found no dangling rope to enable him to board her at that quarter and swam round to the starboard side where he found the ladder.

It was a short swim and for Steve, not in the least fatiguing. He pulled himself up swiftly but as his head appeared above the rail, he was seen by a uniformed seaman who shouted at him.

"Hey, there, you can't come aboard."

Steve swung a leg over the rail and the sailor rushed him. Steve leaped upon the deck, ducked a right swing and brought up his right against the seaman's chin. He jumped over the body of the fellow, plunged toward the companion and appeared suddenly and unexpectedly in the cabin.

JACK CLEWS, WHO was sitting at a writing desk on the port side, glanced up and uttered a startled exclamation and then a gasp as a pair of mighty hands grasped his throat and pulled him out of his chair.

"My bonds, damn you," growled the wild man. Clews could only make a choked sound. Bang! The yacht captain had fired from the hatchway. "Got him," he shouted excitedly.

For luck had abandoned Steve Cobb. The luck which had kept him out of police hands, which had enabled him to escape the bullets of the kidnappers and the shots from the revolver of Hutton had done all that could be expected from it.

Steve toppled over sidewise, carrying Jack Clews to the carpet with him. His bulk crashed heavily but his hands released their grip and Clews struggled to his feet.

"Damn you, you might have hit me," he sputtered. He gazed down upon the giant and a slow smile spread over his face. "Much obliged, at that," he said. He dropped to his knees beside the unconscious man and looked for the wound.

"Creased him," he said looking up at the skipper who stood nervously beside him. "His head's so thick I'm surprised he noticed it."

The bullet had skidded across the top of Steve's head,

causing a scalp wound and stunning the man but no serious damage had been done.

"Top hole," exclaimed Clews. "Couldn't ask anything better."

"I'm glad I didn't kill him," said the skipper with a sigh of relief. "It looked like he was strangling you, sir."

"That shot was heard, so I'm glad we haven't a corpse on our hands. Tie him up. He'll be conscious in a few minutes. Put chains on him. The big gorilla looks as though he could break a rope cable. Chain him and stick him down the hold. I'll go on deck and tell any hick cop who feels called upon to investigate that I took a shot at a sea gull. How did he get aboard?"

"Swam out, sir. Lawson challenged him and he about broke the swab's jaw."

"Get some chains and shove him below. Hurry up."

Clews went on deck and seated himself in the cushioned wicker chair at the stem. "What a break," he chuckled. "Right back where he started from."

He gazed reflectively across the port upon which the sun was beginning to set and which was causing flames, apparently, to dance on the windows of Warburton's big house.

"Right into my hands," he muttered. "And the whole damn game is in my hands. Bill Warburton will howl to the high heavens, but he'll pay through the nose."

24

TWO WOMEN

IT TOOK SEVERAL moments for Lucinda Warburton to recover from her dismay and her anger. Being a young woman who liked to dramatize things, she had been setting the stage as she rested in her chamber for the big scene with Steve Cobb. She was going to watch until she saw him loafing on the beach, his giant frame recumbent as usual.

And Steve would be able to loaf by tomorrow, for her father had promised to do something about the preposterous accusation of murder against him.

She was going to come upon him and touch him with her shoe, just as she had done the first time she saw him. He would open those great eyes of his and grin up at her and then she would make her speech.

She would apologize humbly for all the nasty things she had said to him and tell him she forgave him for the mean things he had said to her and then explain that she had learned all about his stupendous heroism in rescuing her from the criminals.

It would be in character for him to tell her that he would do the same for anybody and it didn't mean a thing, but Lucinda would smile upon him bewitchingly and say:

"Steve, that's nonsense. You did it because you love me

and I want to tell you that I reciprocate your feelings for me."

She was a little vague as to what would follow but it included being squeezed in those big arms and being kissed like the first day only much more passionately.

In the meantime she proposed to tell Diana Warburton what she thought of her for pretending that Steve was her lover and how despicable was her treatment of her husband. With this purpose she had boldly entered her stepmother's room and there was the unspeakable Steve Cobb committing not only burglary but vandalism.

It meant that he couldn't be the white-souled knight she had built him up to be. It meant that there was something between him and Diana after all—and a quarrel had taken place and this was his revenge, perhaps. What had he said about her stepmother? In the attic, all bound up with a woolen string?

Had they been meeting in the attic? It was too awful to contemplate. But what had he meant?

So Lucinda went up the attic stairs and pushed open the door and there was Mrs. Warburton laying upon the old bed which had no sheets or blankets and had a mattress which was almost in shreds. And she was bound all right but with stout rope and there was a gag in her mouth.

Lucinda rushed to the woman and unfastened the cloth around her mouth, saw the end of a handkerchief protruding from the mouth and pulled it out.

"What has happened?" she demanded.

Mrs. Warburton made pitiful sounds but nothing distinguishable. Lucinda whose tender heart caused her to weep at the plight of the woman she hated, endeavored, clumsily, to untie the knots fastened by the strong hands of Steve Cobb.

"Get a knife, you fool," said her stepmother thickly. "Those ropes are killing me."

Lucinda ran towards the door.

"Don't tell anyone," called Mrs. Warburton, but Lucinda slammed the door behind her. In a moment she was back with a hunting knife from her father's room and with a few slashes set the prisoner free.

Mrs. Warburton rolled over on her face, and shook with heavy furious sobs.

"Who did this awful thing?" demanded Lucinda who seated herself beside the suffering woman and stroked her hair. She had to repeat her question three times before she got an answer.

"I don't know," said Mrs. Warburton sullenly. "I came up here out of curiosity and a man pounced on me. I didn't see his face."

Lucinda's eyes flamed. "I did," she said. "It was Steve Cobb."

"It wasn't. How could it be?"

Mrs. Warburton was sitting up. She grasped the girl by the shoulders. "You must be crazy. It was a burglar."

"It was Steve Cobb," said Lucinda. "He told me you were up here all bound around with a woolen string."

"Damn him," cried Diana passionately. "He'll pay for this. How he'll pay for this!"

"So he was your lover, after all. Why did he maltreat you?"

Diana's eyes narrowed. "Will you promise me not to tell this to your father?"

"No."

"All right," said Diana venomously. "We spent the night here. And he demanded money. I refused. He tied me up and went down to rob me of what cash there was in my room."

LUCINDA GREW PALE as death. Steve had been searching Diana's room, tearing things apart in his eagerness to find something. Suddenly her eyes sparkled with anger.

"You lie!" she cried. "You are a wicked contemptible liar. Steve didn't spend the night with you."

"I'm telling you he did."

"And I know he didn't, because it was Steve Cobb who saved me from the kidnappers away up near Plymouth at two o'clock this morning."

With this Lucinda walked straight out of the room.

Diana gazed at her retreating back malevolently. The little fool was in love with Steve Cobb.

Cobb, no doubt was in love with her, which explained his Sir Galahad attitude toward herself.

Well, he was a monstrosity of bone and muscle with no more brains than an ox. She didn't love him any more; she hated him. She would love to see him tortured. If they sentenced him to death, she would like to see him fry in the electric chair.

It was absolutely certain that Lucinda was going straight to her father with her tale. It was most unlikely that her fascination over Warburton would survive this situation. She crossed the room and peered out of the window. The yawl was back.

The time had come to throw off the mask, walk out of this house for good and cast her lot with Jack Clews. And

she had better get going before her husband intercepted
her.

Diana left the attic and hastened to her room, entered,
and emitted a wail of anguish. All her possessions tossed
about. Everything scattered over the rug. Her best dresses a
heap on the closet floor. Perfumes, ointments, beauty helps
of every description in a helter skelter melange.

The devastation here actually hurt her more than her
outrageous personal treatment at the hands of Steve Cobb.
Her lips moved. She was silently cursing him.

Recovering from her first shock she set to work to pack
what she wished to take with her. She'd go to the Inn at
Hyannis with her luggage and notify Jack of her where-
abouts. Warburton would balk at sending her goods out
to the yawl. She was packed in half an hour and then there
was a knock at her door. She opened it. Her husband stood
there. There was rage in his eyes, menace in the expression
of his mouth. She tossed him a glare of defiance.

"Going somewhere?" he asked with heavy irony.

"I'm leaving you, William," she said sullenly.

He nodded. "For five years I've put up with your effron-
tery. It's time you went," he said bitterly. "I'll contest a
divorce suit. I have plenty of evidence of your infidelity.
You'll never touch a cent of my money."

Diana laughed nastily. "I'm leaving you, my dear, because
the way things are shaping up, I don't think you are going
to have any money. In fact I wouldn't be surprised if you
found yourself in jail."

He lifted a clenched fist. "You hussy, what do you mean?"
he shouted.

She laughed even more nastily. "I married you for

your money. You have nothing else to recommend you. I think your chickens are coming home to roost, William. I suppose you'll let me have a car to take me to the Hyannis Inn."

He controlled his temper with difficulty. "It will be a pleasure," he stated. "Good by and good riddance."

TEN MINUTES LATER a Warburton car carried away Mrs. Warburton and a dozen bags and boxes. In Cobbport she stopped long enough to write a note to Jack Clews and hire a boatman to take it to the yawl. As she rode out of the village she did not observe a shriveled and gnarled old man who leaned on a stick and who was standing beside a small, shabby but pretty little girl.

"That's Jezebel," said General Burton. "Take a good look, Myra. Them kind of woman has raised ructions through the ages. Don't you never grow up and get to be like her."

"She's beautiful, though," remarked Myra Sears. "And I'd like to have clothes like hers."

"Those are the wages of sin, Myra."

"Oh, General what do you think's become of Steve?"

"No news is good news," said the old man. "But the orders are out to shoot to kill if he resists and Steve won't surrender. Where is this state detective staying?"

"At Mrs. Joshua Loring's house."

"We'll be going up there."

The girl grasped his arm. "Oh, General, I'm afraid."

" 'Tenshun. Forward march," commanded the General.

25

A GIANT IN CHAINS

"SHOOT TO KILL" were the orders, as it happened. The whole Cape was excited. Local police were on the *qui vive* and state police were coming down by the dozen. Reporters were pouring in and news-camera men. Steve Cobb in a couple of days had created a reputation second only to Dillinger's.

Two and two had been put together to make ten. The fellow was leader of a desperate gang. The crooks who had rescued him from Officer Noonan and Chief Eben Cobb were the quartet killed or wounded by policemen Nutley and Brown of the Plymouth. The leader, murderer, and kidnaper, was at large. He had been seen, according to reports, on every town on the Cape. He was eight feet high and four feet broad and had a face like a devil. Local police and constables walked with their hands in their pockets clutching their guns. Being in mortal terror of the outlaw, they were likely to shoot at him on sight. On the other hand, between their nerves and natural poor marksmanship, it wasn't likely that they would hit him except by accident.

The state officers, of course, were a different breed; hard, cool-headed men who were well-trained and courageous.

These had trailed him back to Cobbport by the array of stolen cars. There was the Packard commandeered at Hyannis found up near Plymouth. The Warburton car, used by the kidnappers had been discovered not far from the Buzzard's Bay end of the Cape Cod Canal. The Ford stolen at Sandwich had been picked up on the Cobbport road outside the village.

There were few good hiding places in the vicinity of Cobbport. Vegetation on Cape Cod is sparse; the woods are of scrub pine, there are few caves—nature there is not well disposed toward fugitives. As he was known to be a remarkable swimmer, it was thought he might have swum out to one of the many islands off the shore and officers in motor boats were moving from island to island. It was confidently expected that Steve would be captured in twenty-four hours.

Every house in Cobbport was entered during the day and not even Warburton's was overlooked. However at Warburton's, a statement of the butler that no such person was within was accepted without question. In view of the fact that Cobb had kidnaped Warburton's daughter it was considered highly improbable that he would present himself there.

About six P.M., the green yawl Emerald cast loose from her moorings and, as there was no wind, she left the Haven on her auxiliary engine. She jogged down the coast a few miles to Hyannisport.

Half an hour later, a rowboat conveyed a dark beautiful young woman in yachting costume out to the Emerald. She was met at the ladder by a big man in whites wearing a yachting cap who was John Clews, owner of the craft.

"Hello, Diana," he said cheerfully. "You decided that it was time to make the break, eh?"

"Wait till you hear what I have to tell you and you'll understand," she said significantly.

He laughed gaily. "I've something quite interesting to tell you, old girl. Lets go down to the cabin and open a bottle of wine."

The hold of the yawl was small and congested. The ventilation was negligible and it was horribly hot. Steve Cobb sat upon a box of canned goods in the dark. There were chains around his ankles and a couple of lengths of chain pinioned his arms to his side. They hadn't bothered to feed him and he was in a state of impotent fury. Hours had passed, long stuffy hours in which he had opportunity for introspection which did him no good, for it only showed him his folly in all the colors of the rainbow.

He was sunk in sullen despair when he heard a bolt over his head being thrust back, and the hatch was lifted. Light streamed down, and a pair of beautiful silk clad legs appeared on the ladder to the hold.

In a couple of seconds a woman stood before him. There was enough light from above to inform him of her identity.

"Hello, Diana," he said coolly. Clews dropped down the ladder and stood beside her, a gun in his hand. "Don't try to start anything, Cobb," he warned.

"And how do you like being tied up, you rat?" demanded the woman shrilly. "Jack, why didn't you gag him the way he did me?"

"Not necessary. Nobody can hear shouts from this place," replied the yachtsman.

"But I want him to suffer," she cried. "Steve Cobb, I hate you! I despise you!"

SHE STEPPED FORWARD, clenched her little fist and struck him in the right cheek.

Clews grabbed her roughly and pulled her back.

"None of that," he said sternly. "You promised to behave yourself."

Tears of anger spurted from her eyes. "I hate him so," she sobbed.

"You'll be interested to learn, Cobb," said Clews, "that the police will shoot you on sight, if you go ashore. The papers are calling you the 'Mad Man of Cape Cod.' One of them referred to you as the 'Naked Savage.' Rather appropriate, eh?"

Steve made no answer.

"I'm a business man," said Clews. "I've nothing against you but you would have been wise to agree to my terms last night. In the public state of mind you'll be sentenced for murder without the jury leaving its seat. I've got you where I want you, Cobb. You have no choice but do business with me."

"See you damned first," said Steve loudly.

Diana lifted a flashlight and turned it on the prisoner. "Look at him," she said contemptuously. "Look at that stupid jaw. You can't reason with the brute and we don't need him any more."

Steve inspected his surroundings as the woman turned the flashlight curiously upon the contents of the hold. He observed a stout hook driven into a heavy timber above his head; evidently intended to hang a side of beef for a brief period. His eyes snapped with interest.

"I've been in communication with Warburton," said Clews. "We're meeting at his place tonight at eleven. If I convince him that I have the bonds and that you are my prisoner, we'll reach an agreement. He has to accept my terms."

"I can prove ownership of the bonds," said Steve. "So what?"

"There is so much money in this I can afford to be generous. Conditions have changed, though. I'll pay you a hundred thousand for the bonds. Agree and I'll sail you up to Canada and get you on a liner for Europe."

"If not—"

"You'll come to a well deserved end," cried Diana viciously.

"Murder, eh?"

"You killed Hutton, didn't you? The State will execute you. I'll have to save the State all the expense and bother of a trial."

"Well," said Steve. "This is as good a time as any and you both bore me frightfully. Get busy."

Diana screamed furiously. "I'll tear your eyes out."

She rushed at him, claws extended. Clews grasped her by the back of the neck and pulled her back.

"Get up the ladder," he commanded harshly. "I think Cobb will eventually listen to reason."

"You thinking of marrying that hellcat?" inquired Steve insolently.

Clews disdained to answer, but forced Diana up the ladder, followed her and slammed down the hatch cover. Steve heard two bolts being shot.

He sat thoughtfully on his box for a few minutes. In

the dark he had been unable to get a notion of his prison but now he had an excellent picture of it. He hadn't had a chance to inspect his chains but they had been stout enough to resist his efforts to break them.

They were light chains—the yawl wasn't equipped like a jail. If he had been smart enough to exhale when he was being bound, he might have broken those around his arms and chest by expansion. As he was semi-conscious when the skipper had chained him, he couldn't be expected to think of everything.

HE STOOD UP. He could move his wrists and fingers and, while he couldn't walk, he could hop. He got hold of the edge of a packing case with one hand and, by using his strength, dragged it slowly, hopping beside it, until he judged it was beneath the hook he had observed in the cross timber of the yawl.

He then sat on the box, drew up his knees and got his feet upon the edge of it. He pushed himself back a foot and then began the ticklish business of standing up with ankles bound and arms fastened to his side. He was almost upright when he lost his balance and fell to the deck. He went through the whole process again and this time was successful, but he had to bend almost double as the hold was only seven feet high, the packing case was two feet high and Steve was six feet four. This accomplished, he began to feel for the hook with his shoulders and finally located it.

The next step took much time and infinite patience. Being without arms he had to manage to get the chain across his back over the point of the hook. It must have been half an hour before he finally had succeeded in hook-

Steve was on his feet—
the automatic barked.

ing himself and Steve perspired like a stevedore after eight hours in the hot sun.

Everything now depended upon the strength of the hook. He threw his great weight and strength against the chain. He strained every nerve and muscle. For a few seconds the result was in doubt and then the chain broke and Steve pitched off the packing case and landed heavily upon the deck.

But his arms were free. It was a matter of a few minutes to free his legs. There were no locks on these chains. The skipper had pulled them tight and knotted them. Steve's powerful fingers triumphed and he was no longer bound, but he was still a prisoner.

He rested for a while after this accomplishment. If the fools had used ropes, he would still have been tied up.

After a while, he made the next move. He placed the packing case under the hatch cover and brought his powerful back into play against it. For five minutes he pushed until even his stout heart couldn't stand the strain. It was a heavy wooden cover and the bolts securing it were not to be forced.

He lay down flat on the deck to recuperate. As he was free he could jump on Clews, if he came back into the hold. But Clews was going ashore, he might already have gone. Clews and Warburton might reach an agreement and destroy the bonds. Anyway he had to get out of here and quickly.

There was another expedient but one so desperate so perilous that even reckless Steve Cobb hesitated to make use of it. It was highly probable that he would be condemning himself to death and conferring a great favor on Clews and Warburton.

ANYWAY, HE MUST wait at least another hour to make sure that the yawl owner had gone ashore. Having no means of telling time, he began to count seconds. Thirty-six hundred seconds made an hour. As he would probably count too fast he would count up to seven thousand seconds.

At fifty-five hundred seconds he broke off. "Now or never," he muttered. Groping his way across the hold he fumbled about and grunted when he found what he was looking for.

"Probably caught like a rat in a trap," he said aloud and opened the sea-cock.

The water began to enter the hold. It rushed in steadily and in a thick stream, but it seemed an age before Steve felt it swirling round his ankles. Grimly, he waited. Slowly it climbed to his knees. It forced its way through partitions and was filling the entire hold of the yawl. It was a couple of inches above his knees. Steve who had picked up one of the chains which had bound him, climbed on the packing case and began to beat with the chain against the hatch cover.

Several things might happen. She might capsize. In that case he was doomed. She might settle on an even keel and be on the point of sinking before the crew realized it, in which case they would abandon her in great haste, forgetful of the prisoner. Or they might notice that she was filling soon enough to open the hatchway and release him.

For several minutes he pounded frantically while the water rose steadily and the yawl creaked and groaned as though aware of her fate. It came upon him that they had forgotten him and fled from the doomed yacht. Death by drowning. It wouldn't be so bad in the open sea but in this foul hole—

Clunk. Clunk. The bolts. The hatch cover was lifted. Steve leaped out upon the upper deck.

The yacht captain stood there.

"Damn you, you opened the seacock," he roared. He had a gun in his hand which he made to lift. Steve tore it away from him.

"Let's get out of this," he said with a mad laugh. "She'll sink in five minutes."

"Your chains, where are they?" stammered the man who was so astonished and frightened that he wasn't dangerous.

"Oh, I broke them," said Steve. He grasped the captain, a middle-aged heavy man who was uncertain what to do under the circumstances about this naked brute who broke chains and dared to sink a ship, and ran with him out of the deck house.

The deck was within a few inches of being level with the sea. Steve glanced ashore and recognized, by its arrangement of lights, Hyannisport. There was a boat waiting with three men at the oars.

"Get abroad," commanded the skipper.

"You are still Mr. Clews' prisoner."

Steve covered him with the revolver. "Get aboard and shove off," he commanded.

"But you'll drown."

"Don't be silly."

He watched the boat leave the port side and then went overboard from the starboard side.

The boat pulled steadily for the pier and it was evident that the captain didn't care to pursue the naked man with the revolver.

If the skipper knew his identity he'd set the police after him as soon as he landed, unaware that capture by the police was the last thing Clews wished to happen to Steve Cobb.

He kept glancing over his shoulder as he headed for an uninhabited stretch of shore and finally he saw the Emerald disappear beneath the surface of the bay. He dropped the revolver and struck out lustily.

"Well, I hope she's not insured," he muttered maliciously. "Considering everything, I'd like Clews to stand the loss."

At that moment a church-bell began to boom the hour. He counted. Nine o'clock.

"I guess I'll have plenty of time," remarked Steve Cobb.

26

MISGUIDED FRIENDS

STATE OFFICER NOONAN sat with a bandaged shoulder in a big cushioned wicker chair in the bedroom which he was occupying in the cottage of Mrs. Joshua Loring.

Myra Sears and the General could see him through the window and they saw that he was not alone. William Warburton and Lucinda were with him.

"See," said Myra. "We can't go in now."

But the General rang the bell and Mrs. Loring opened the door. "General," she exclaimed. "Imagine you coming calling." She tittered.

"We got important business with Mr. Noonan," said the ancient stiffly.

"Well, come in and set. Mr. and Miss Warburton are with him now, but I guess they won't be long."

"Me and Myra ain't in a hurry."

The General seated himself painfully and Myra squatted on the sofa.

"What can they do to me? Put me in jail?" she demanded.

"I told you they can't do nothin'. Be still, I got thinkin' to do."

"Now, Mr. Warburton," the State officer was saying, "you are absolutely certain Cobb didn't know the dead man?"

"I'm quite certain of it."

"And you say that you sent him to see Cobb to make him a business offer."

Warburton nodded. Lucinda smiled with satisfaction.

"I had endeavored to talk to Cobb personally," said the millionaire. "But he said he wasn't interested in business any more. I decided to make him a detailed proposition through a third party. Sales manager at a salary of fifteen thousand a year."

"Well, well. A man would feel pretty kindly toward a person who came with a proposition like that."

"He certainly wouldn't kill him."

"I was arresting him on suspicion," said Noonan. "On account of Myra Sears' statement that she heard voices and saw lights in the house while Cobb denied that there had been anybody there. What makes it black for him is the fact that he was rescued by the kidnapers who carried off your daughter. He certainly is a criminal and that makes it look like he might have killed Hutton and robbed him—not knowing he came with a bona fide offer of big money."

"While I told the officers I wouldn't repeat the facts," said Warburton "the truth is that Brown and Nutley confessed to me privately that they had lied about the affair on the Plymouth road. Steve Cobb saw my daughter in the kidnapers' car as they left my estate. Lucinda called for help. He secured a car—if he stole it, it's a slight offense under the circumstances, pursued, overtook the kidnapers and, single-handed, overpowered them.

"The officers arrived on the scene, and accused him of stealing the car, whereupon he disarmed them, made them take Lucinda into Plymouth and returned to the Cape."

"Say," cried Noonan excitedly, "that's damn funny. You say these cops told you this tale themselves?"

"I forced it out of them. They took credit for the rescue hoping that the supposed criminal would never dare to contradict them."

"Steve Cobb is about the most wonderful person in the world," said Lucinda firmly. "And he wouldn't hurt a fly."

"Well," replied the detective. "He probably didn't consider these gunmen he killed under the heading of flies. If it wasn't for resisting arrest and me getting shot up, the case against Cobb in the Hutton killing wouldn't look strong at all. Who do you suppose killed Hutton?"

Warburton smiled maliciously. "We know that the four men who carried off my daughter were lurking in the vicinity."

Noonan nodded. "That's so," he agreed. "Begins to look like they might have done it. Just the same I've got to find Cobb and talk with him. Know where he is?"

"I have no idea," replied Warburton.

"You mean you'll let Steve go?" demanded Lucinda eagerly.

"Well, I'll have to hold him a few days. If you know where he is, Miss, you tell him to come in. People think he's a homicidal maniac and he's liable to get shot in his tracks."

"I—I wish I knew where he was," she said dolefully.

"Well, we'll be going. Come dear," said Warburton to his daughter.

Noonan thanked them and sighed. The case against Steve Cobb looked as though it had gone a glimmering.

Warburton opened the door.

"Why, General!" Lucinda exclaimed. "Oh, Mr. Noonan,

the General was with Steve when I hollered from the car. He heard me. General, it was Steve who pursued us, wasn't it?"

"Hello, Lucinda," said the old man, beaming. "Steve went after you hell bent for election."

"So there," said Lucinda to the detective.

She passed out of the house with her father and Mrs. Loring conducted the General and Myra into the detective's chamber.

"Hello, Myra," said Noonan pleasantly. "Glad to meet you, General Burton. I've heard about you."

"Everybody's heard about me," retorted the General. "Only bona fide hundred and one year old person in the United States. All the others are fakes."

"What can I do for you? Sit down, sir."

"I come here," said the General pompously, "to prove that while Steve Cobb killed this Hutton, it was a clear case of justifiable homicide."

Noonan's eyes sharpened and he sucked in his breath.

"You don't say!" he exclaimed. "And how are you going to prove it?"

The General pointed his attenuated forefinger at Myra. "By her," he declared.

"But Myra has already told all she knows."

THE OLD MAN cackled. "Not by a long shot. You see, Mr. Noonan, she didn't want to get Steve into trouble and, not being any judge of evidence, she was afraid to tell what she knowed. I sez to her, 'You got to give your evidence, Myra. Any man has a right to defend himself and they can't do nothin' to Steve.'"

"They can't, can they?" asked Myra anxiously.

"Hump. Probably not," said the detective cautiously. He suppressed his eagerness. First Warburton had endeavored to persuade him that Hutton had been unknown to Cobb and had been bringing him glad tidings. Noonan had been almost persuaded that Steve couldn't possibly have killed Hutton. And now had come along two simpletons who admitted the killing.

"Now, Myra," he said, "suppose you tell me what you ought to have told me last night."

"Well," said Myra, "I woke up and I saw a light in Steve's house so I went up on the hill where he was asleep and woke him up. He told me to go home but I'm awful fond of Steve and I was afraid something might happen to him so I sort of sneaked after him."

"And then what? Go on."

"Well, I went around to the front of the house, keeping far enough back so Steve wouldn't know I was following him."

"Yes, yes."

"And I was right in front of the door when Steve went in, only down the lane a bit. And I saw big flashes of fire come out of the house and Steve fall down and I got scared and ran."

"Flashes of fire? Like a gun?"

"Yes, only there wasn't any report like a gun."

"And then what did you do?"

"I saw the light go on in Steve's house and I was frightened he had been hurt and I had to find out so I went back, kind of slowly. Just before I got there, the light went out. I heard moving around in there, like bumping. I yelled in to Steve. He said there was nobody there and nothing was stolen and told me to go to bed. He sounded cross so I went."

"What else do you know?"

"That's all."

"Then how do you know he killed somebody?"

"I—I don't. The General said so."

"Ah," cried the detective. "And how do you know, old man?" He pointed his finger at the ancient.

"Who me?" demanded the General, suddenly confused. "I don't know nothin'."

"You said he killed Hutton in self-defense. How do you know?"

"I'm an old man," muttered Burton. "I—I just suppose so."

"You'll go to jail if you don't tell the truth. You won't live long in jail."

"I—I just put two and two together," said the General sullenly. "Stands to reason this feller shot at Steve. I've heard they have some contraption on guns to make 'em silent. And Steve hit him too hard."

"But you didn't see this killing?"

"No sir-ee. I was asleep on the beach, I was."

"Myra, you're certain there was somebody in the house with Cobb?"

"Yes, sir," she said, on the point of tears.

"You claimed you heard voices—"

"I thought I did. I ain't sure."

"Why didn't you tell the truth last night?"

"I didn't want to get Steve into trouble," she said frankly. He scowled at her.

"But you knew he was guilty, you pretended to faint and you went out your window to warn him."

Myra began to weep. Noonan who was kind hearted patted her on the head.

"Well, well; that's all. Don't worry. You're all right."

"And so is Steve, isn't he, Mr. Noonan?"

"Oh, sure," replied the detective. "I've made notes of your statements, you two, so don't try to deny them. You can go now."

"Yes, sir." The General got himself upon his feeble legs. "A man has a right to defend himself against a burglar," he stated. "Supposing Steve did kill this feller after he was shot at, it ain't murder."

"How did Hutton's body get out into the middle of the ocean?" demanded Noonan.

"I don't know nothin' about that," said the General hastily. "Come along Myra."

AFTER THE PAIR had departed, Noonan grabbed paper and began to transcribe his notes. He was grinning with satisfaction. As he had informed Warburton, his case against Steve Cobb had been very wobbly. There was no motive for the killing, apparently. There was nothing but a presumption that Hutton had actually visited Cobb. The fellow had a good reputation. Some village loafer might have been in Cobb's house, assuming Myra Sears hadn't imagined what she had said. Myra hadn't seen Hutton at all.

But now he had a case. Warburton admitted sending Hutton to call on Cobb. Myra had seen flashes of a gun with a silencer on it, fired by somebody inside the house as Cobb entered. Cobb had lied to her when he said nobody had been there. Hutton had died from a blow on the temple and Cobb was big and strong enough to strike a death blow.

And Cobb had thrown the body into the sea instead of standing on his rights as a householder, which was an indication of guilt.

It was probable that Warburton, influenced by Cobb's rescue of his daughter had skidded around the truth. Noonan knew that Warburton had taken the Cobb family business away from Steve's father. Suppose he had sent Hutton with a threat of some sort instead of an offer of employment. That would supply a motive.

Noonan's business was to find the killer of Hutton and bring him in. Under what circumstances the pair had met, and what Steve's motives for killing the man might be, was something to be brought out in the trial. Thanks to the statements of the old man and the young girl, he had evidence of a battle at the hut. The old General knew more than he had admitted but what he knew could easily be scared out of him.

Noonan admitted that the bullet in the doorjamb indicated by its position that it had been fired from inside the house, which bore out Myra's statement that four flashes had been seen as Steve entered. Cobb, perhaps, had dropped, avoided the bullets, and then closed with the man and knocked him lifeless. If, as Warburton claimed, Steve had attacked and eliminated four kidnapers, he was quite a person. Noonan had rather liked him at their only meeting. However, Cobb had killed Hutton and he'd have to stand trial for the killing. The thing to do was to catch him.

It was queer how Cobb had fought the mob which

had forcibly rescued him; he hadn't acted as though they were friends he had been expecting. Well, whether he was convicted or acquitted was none of State officer Noonan's business. He had to get the killer of Frank Hutton.

He thought whimsically that he wouldn't care to live to be a hundred and one years old in his line of work, the chances were against it. He wondered how Steve had won the love and loyalty of the ancient man and the fifteen year old girl. He must be a pretty good fellow when he wasn't riled. That Lucinda Warburton certainly seemed to think a lot of him and she was the best looking doll who had crossed Mr. Noonan's path in many a long day.

27

BIRDS OF A FEATHER

"DAD," SAID LUCINDA as she snuggled beside her father in the car outside Mrs. Loring's door, "you're a trump."

"Thanks, dear," he said absently.

"Now that she's gone, we'll be pals together, won't we?"

"Yes. Certainly."

"You won't ever let her come back again, will you?"

"No," he said firmly.

"She's awfully fascinating, though. And half a dozen times you were going to get rid of her but you weakened."

"She's gone too far this time," he said grimly.

"Now that she's gone, I've a mind to tell you something. I didn't before because I didn't want to hurt you."

"What, Lucinda?"

"That night you found S-Steve in her room. She hadn't been in the house half an hour?"

"You mean she was with him?" asked Warburton dully.

Lucinda shook her head. "She left the house early in the evening. She was out on that green yawl with that awful Mr. Clews."

"Are you sure?"

"Yes. And last night, too. I saw her rowing out there before eight o'clock. She's a wicked woman, father."

Warburton's hands clenched tightly on the driving wheel. He stopped the car before the entrance of his house, helped out his daughter, and said, "I'm going to be busy in the library all evening, child. I have a business meeting with Clews at eleven.

"I'm glad you confided in me. I had no notion that Diana was on very friendly terms with the fellow."

He shut himself into the library and dropped heavily into a chair. The man was suffering intensely. Although he had practically put Diana out of the house, he was experiencing the pangs of jealousy. Diana and Clews!

The woman had boasted of her amours and, if he had had any spirit, he would have driven her forth long ago but it had never occurred to him that she might betray his business secrets. Her attitude toward business had always been one of complete disinterest.

Yet he was confident that nobody in his office except the auditor and himself knew of the existence of the original small issue of Cobb bonds. He had confided in Hutton but Hutton had left the house, had had no private conversation with Diana and gone straight to his death.

Cobb, of course, owning the bonds, knew their value. Had he told Diana about it? Warburton didn't agree with Lucinda that there was nothing between Steve and Diana. She was a woman capable of several love affairs simultaneously. It was possible that the young fool had boasted to Diana of the menace the bonds were to her husband's plans and she, scenting big money, had let Clews into the secret.

It was certain that Clews had learned about the securities from the viper Warburton had been nursing at his bosom. A man ought to be allowed to kill a woman like that. Clews, his wife's lover, proposed to walk in and black-mail her husband. Ethically Warburton had a right to lay him dead at his feet but the law didn't look at things that way.

He busied himself going over the prospectus for the new stock issues. There wasn't a proposition in America as promising.

The banks were full of money, eager to make safe invest-ments; there was a vast profit at hand and freedom from indebtedness. Damn Clews and damn Steve Cobb.

He opened a small ledger and for an hour was immersed in calculations. If it proved necessary to do business with Clews, he had to find out exactly how much he could pay and keep his head above the waters of finance.

There was a discreet knock at the door. The butler entered.

"Mr. John Clews calling, sir," said the man. "He states that he has an appointment with you."

"Show him in," said Warburton. "Wait. You can go to bed, I'll let him out myself."

"Yes, sir. Thank you, sir."

A moment later the yachtsman came jauntily into the library. The eyes of the two men met like swords clashing but both were well bred, both loved money more than anything else and each wished to observe the amenities.

"Good evening, Mr. Clews," said Warburton who had risen. "Take a chair. Have a spot of liquor?"

"No, thanks."

CLEWS DROPPED INTO a chair beside the big library table and let his eyes rove around the room. It was an immense room, with a huge fireplace at one end and bookshelves on one long wall. The symmetry of the room was marred by one corner having been cut off.

"Rather curious, that," commented the visitor.

"Yes. Old Cobb sacrificed to convenience. He stuck a bar in that corner of the room. There was a door giving admittance to it from the library but he had it removed and the partition papered over. If I should decide to make this a permanent summer residence, I'd pull the damn thing out." He smiled politely. The pair might have been friends and this a social call, judging by their pretense.

"I trust your daughter is quite recovered," said Clews.

"Quite."

"And Mrs. Warburton?" he asked blandly.

Warburton flushed. "She has left my bed and board," he said flatly.

Clews' manner displayed polite astonishment. "Ah, a pity. I trust there will be a reconciliation."

"There will not be a reconciliation." Warburton was having trouble with his naturally quick temper. "Suppose we get to the object of your visit."

"You'll pardon me if I look round?"

Clews rose walked swiftly to a closet, pulled it open and inspected it. Returning, he looked under the table.

"There are no dictaphones and no witnesses to this conference," said Warburton.

Clews sat down in his former chair. Warburton pulled his chair close to the table.

"I have something that you want," said Clews. "It's a question of price."

"You probably exaggerate my need of those securities,"

countered the other, "and you will have to prove that you can deliver."

"I can. I know exactly your situation. These freak bonds have a death grip on the Cobb Company. They not only prevent you from re-financing but may compel you to pay into the treasury of the company several millions in dividends paid by Ezra Cobb upon illegally issued preferred and common stock. You owe five millions to the banks, mostly on demand notes. If a rumor gets afloat you can't put out the new Cobb securities, the notes will be called and you can't meet them."

"You are mistaken," said Warburton hurriedly. "I have the best legal advice and I am informed that the restrictions specified in those bonds are indefensible, and won't stand in the courts."

"Possibly. They seem harsh. If you can wait a couple of years before re-financing, you may find your attorney's opinions upheld—and you may not."

"Please state your proposition."

"For two hundred fifty thousand in cash and a contract to purchase for two and a quarter millions, I'll sell you the bonds."

Warburton turned pale. "Preposterous. I haven't any such money."

"You'll make a five million profit upon the underwriters' price for your securities after paying off your firm indebtedness. I'm only asking half. Refuse and I'll bankrupt you by applying for an injunction against Cobb re-financing."

"You forget that the bonds are not your property. You have no title."

"What you want to do is to retire the bonds quietly."

"THAT'S THE OBVIOUS thing to do but it's impossible. Young Cobb can prove ownership. A protest from him will prevent anything like that. You've nothing to sell, Mr. Clews."

"Young Cobb will prove nothing."

"I'm paying no money on your say so, Mr. Clews. I don't even know if you have the bonds."

"I'll settle that doubt." Clews drew from the breast pocket of his linen suit a package of engraved papers shifted them to his left hand and drew from his hip a heavy automatic which he laid in front of him on the library table.

"You may inspect them," he said, passing over the bonds.

With a hand which trembled, Warburton grasped the bonds, thrust his eyeglasses upon his nose and eagerly inspected them. Clews wore a complacent smile.

"Those are the bonds," admitted Warburton who reluctantly laid them upon the table. "There are records, however, of the interest having been paid to Cobb over a term of years. His ownership is unquestioned. You can't sell me stolen property, Clews."

Clews lighted himself a cigarette and puffed with a satisfied manner.

"As I figure it out," he said, "you sent Hutton to kill Cobb and steal the bonds. If he had succeeded you would have retired the bonds as of the date of your settlement with his father six months ago."

"I—I deny that," cried Warburton shakily.

"I'm not interested. We're alone here. If Cobb had met with an accident, say, and the bonds came into your possession, that is the course you would have followed."

"Admitting the premise, yes."

"It may interest you to know that Steve Cobb is in the hold of my yawl, chained fast. If his body is found on the beach with a couple of bullet holes in it, no questions will be asked. He's a wild man and the police orders are to shoot to kill."

"I—I make no murder pact with you," muttered Warburton who was perspiring. "I don't believe your statement. Cobb was in Cobbport early this evening. I happen to know that."

"And the ass swam out to the yawl and tried to recover his bonds. He walked right into my hands."

"It—it's hard to believe."

"Warburton," said Clews. "I'm the same kind of man you are. I keep inside the law. I hate violence. But when millions are the reward, what's the life of a fool? That's the way you look at it. That's the way I look at it."

"I need those bonds, but I'm damned if I pay your price."

"I'll be generous. Two million. The bonds remain in my possession until I'm fully paid. You go ahead with your stock issues. My interests are bound up with yours. Tomorrow morning, when you have proof that a certain obstacle has been removed, we shall go to New York together."

The phone on the library table rang. Warburton answered it.

"For you," he said curtly. Clews picked up the instrument.

"Clews speaking."

"This is Captain Hobbs," cried an excited male voice. "The prisoner got away. He sank the yawl. We had to let him out. He disarmed me."

"All right, all right," said Clews and hung up. He was white as a ghost and his mouth had sagged horribly.

"You seem to be perturbed," said Warburton. "May I ask?"

Crash!

"By God," shouted Clews. His eyes were fixed upon the bar-room partition. It was shaking, quivering and bulging.

Warburton whirled and stared, his eyes sticking out of his head.

"EAVESDROPPERS, EH?" CRIED Clews. "No dictaphones. Living ears! By God—" He reached quickly for his automatic.

There was a terrific crash, the bar-room wall burst open and a huge naked figure plunged into the room.

"Cobb!" shouted Warburton. It is probable that his movement was involuntary but he thrust out both hands and grasped the bonds which lay on the table.

"No, you don't," bellowed the terrified, bewildered and temporarily demented yachtsman. But Warburton, clutching the bonds in his left pulled open the table drawer and lifted a weapon from it.

Cobb was on his feet and rushing across the big room. Clews' eyes turned from that menace and observed the weapon in Warburton's hand. He released the safety catch and his automatic barked three times. The bullets entered Warburton's body. Clews turned his weapon on Steve Cobb and fired but he had no time to aim, three more bullets went wide and then Steve had him by the throat and carried him down to the floor.

Crash, smash, went his big fists into the face of the yachtsman. Crash, smash, bang. He was belaboring an unconscious form when the butler, followed by Lucinda in her night robe and two terrified women servants, poured into the room.

"Father!" shrieked Lucinda and rushed to her parent who lay face down on the floor.

Her voice brought Steve to his senses. He rose to his feet and gazed sullenly down upon the battered and almost lifeless John Clews.

"Steve Cobb, you've killed my father!" cried Lucinda in whose voice was horror and poignant distress.

"No, I didn't, honest I didn't," said Steve earnestly. "He did. This man here. I saw him do it."

"I'll call a doctor and the police," muttered the butler who rushed from the room.

Steve pushed Lucinda aside, lifted Warburton and laid him on a big red leather couch. Warburton had a bullet in the shoulder and in his right side and one in the chest but he wasn't dead. His heart was beating feebly. Lucinda dropped on her knees at his side, weeping loudly. Steve went back and picked up a number of pieces of engraved paper from the floor.

Having no clothes on, he had no place to conceal them so he opened the table drawer and placed them in it. After that he knelt beside Clews who was still out, whose features had been flattened, but whose heart was beating almost normally.

The situation looked bleak, in his opinion. Clews would accuse him of shooting Warburton. With another murder charge against him, his protests wouldn't carry much weight. Anyway, he'd make the police take charge of his bonds.

He went over to Lucinda and lifted her to her feet.

"I swear I didn't do it, dear," he said. "I was listening to them in the bar. They had property of mine and they were bargaining about it. I broke through the wall, Clews drew a gun and fired at me, but he hit your father."

"Don't speak to me," she said stormily.

"Don't ever speak to me again."

Steve went over and sat in a chair and waited. He didn't have long to wait. The butler came in accompanied by two State officers and Eben Cobb, the chief of police, all with guns in their hands.

"I'm unarmed and I surrender," said Steve. They swooped upon him. He extended his arms and submitted to handcuffs.

"I want to call your attention," he said, "to certain bonds in the table drawer where I just placed them. I can prove they are my property and I want you officers to take possession of them."

"So you killed a couple of more people, eh?" said one of the officers roughly. "Well, you'll fry and that's certain."

"I demand that you arrest John Clews, who's laying there on the floor. He shot Warburton."

One of the officers laughed rudely.

"If Warburton recovers consciousness, he'll bear out my statement," said Steve loudly.

28

STEVE'S DECISION

"COME ON," **COMMANDED** the other. "No fairy tales out of you."

Lucinda rushed across the room. "He's telling the truth," she cried. "Father is conscious. He says Clews was the man who shot him."

"Well," said the first officer. "We got plenty on this bird. We'll take 'em both along."

As Steve was leaving with Clews who, though groggy, was able to walk, Dr. Brown bustled in with his bag. They took Steve to the town lock-up and, having no confidence in its ability to hold the mancled giant, they placed an officer with a gun ready in the cell with him. Steve lay down on the cot and immediately fell asleep. It had been another big day.

He was awakened by a touch on the shoulder, the following morning about nine a.m. Eben Cobb had a suit of clothes procured from Steve's house across his arm.

"You're to dress, Steve," he said, "and it's been arranged for you to go up to Warburton's house. He wants to see you."

"Hello, Eben. Still got your whiskers, eh? Then Warburton is alive?"

"Yes, but the Doc only gives him a day or two. Big specialists came over by plane from New York but they agree he can't live. Doc Brown knows what he's talking about all right."

There was a battery of cameras, half a dozen reporters and as many officers outside the lock-up when they brought Steve out. Four officers with drawn weapons escorted the handcuffed young man to the Warburton residence.

Warburton lay in his big bed looking like a ghost but he smiled when Steve entered the room with his escort. Lucinda sat beside his bed and gazed at Steve gravely but said nothing.

"You officers please wait outside," requested Warburton. "I have nothing to fear from Mr. Cobb. Lucinda, please leave us together."

"But, father—"

"Please, dear."

Bowing coldly to Steve, the girl left the room. Cobb seated himself beside the bed.

"Cobb," said Warburton in a firm but weak voice. "I'm not going to recover. I'm glad I've lived long enough to clear you of the charge of killing me."

"So am I," said Steve dryly. He had every reason to hate this man and he was confident that he was getting his just deserts. If Warburton had caused the death of Ezra Cobb by poisoning, he deserved the electric chair. However, the helplessness of the old man had its effect on him. He was glad somebody else had brought him low.

"I have confessed to the police," continued Warburton, "that you had certain securities in your possession which while legally yours, I considered ethically mine. I told them I had sent Hutton to take them away from you and explained that Hutton, being caught in your house, had probably shot at you and you had killed him in self-defense."

"Thank you. I don't believe they could have convicted me."

"I am grateful to you for saving Lucinda from the kidnapers."

"I heard your entire conversation with Clews last night."

The man's face was contorted with shame. For a few seconds he didn't speak.

"I can't make you understand how the necessities of business warp a man," he said. "I faced ruin, the destruction of a vast enterprise. I was half crazy. I thought I had to have those bonds. It seems so unimportant now."

"Warburton," said Steve gravely. "I have reason to believe you had my father poisoned. There can be no truce between you and me."

"That's not true," the man said in a voice which cracked with earnestness. "I gave Hutton carte blanche. I never knew what he had done though he insinuated afterwards that I had instructed him to eliminate your father. His death was a surprise to me. I swear it."

"I'd like to give you the benefit of the doubt."

Warburton swallowed hard. "The game is in your hands," he said. "This morning, I wired my office to issue the new Cobb securities.

"Otherwise my indebtedness cannot be liquidated, the Cobb Company will collapse, and Lucinda will be penniless. Did you hear Clews's proposition to me?"

"Yes."

"He wanted half of my fortune. I'll make the same terms to you."

"I'll think it over," said Steve. "Is that all you have to say?"

"I'll feel much easier in my mind if I know your decision. I'll die more peacefully."

Steve rose. "I don't think you deserve to die peacefully," he said.

Warburton's pale face turned gray. "I can't contradict you," he said sadly.

STEVE ROSE AND walked toward the door. He lifted his handcuffed hands to knock. He hesitated. He walked back to the bed.

"How much does Lucinda know about this bond business?" he asked harshly.

"My God, man, I couldn't tell her."

"How does Mrs. Warburton benefit by this arrangement?"

"Not at all. I cut her out of my will two years ago for good reasons."

"Issue your securities. I'll make no protest."

He went to the door and knocked. The officers entered and took him out to the car. The car conveyed him to the county jail. He learned of the death of Warburton and the departure of Lucinda with her father's body to New York. He lay in the jail four weeks and then was brought up for trial at the county seat.

The trial was by no means the ordeal it might have been because Steve Cobb, as one thing after another leaked out, had come to be something of a popular hero.

Officers Nutley and Brown went on the stand and

testified that they had stolen the credit for the rescue of Lucinda Warburton. They had been forced to do this by a death bed statement regarding that affair from William Warburton. There was also produced a statement from Warburton to the effect that he had sent Hutton to Cobb's house illegally to procure certain documents. A celebrated attorney sat with Steve's lawyer who had been appointed by the State and whispered in his ear. Steve's action in turning the body of Hutton over to the sea was explained to the jury as the natural terror of a young man who had accidentally killed a housebreaker and feared he could not justify his action without witnesses.

The jury acquitted him after fifteen minutes of deliberation and Steve returned by the first train to Cobbport. His bonds were in a safe deposit box. He knew well enough that Warburton's money had greased the wheels of justice and sent the celebrated attorney to aid in his defense but he had received no word from Lucinda Warburton and heard that after her father's death she had sailed for the West Indies.

He didn't blame her. Warburton had been too cowardly to confess his crimes to his daughter and wild horses wouldn't draw an explanation out of Steve.

Clews still lay in the county jail, charged with the murder of William Warburton and Steve was warned not to leave the State as he was the chief witness for the prosecution. He went back to Cobbport and to his little house. The day he arrived, he found a letter from Pennypacker asking him what he proposed to do about the bonds. Steve grinned, tore up the letter and decided not to answer it. He didn't propose to do anything but he had no objections to Penny-packer worrying about the matter.

He knew that the re-financing of the Cobb Company had been a great success and that his father's enterprise was bigger and more profitable than ever and most of the profits were going into the bank account of Lucinda Warburton. He took off his clothes, put on his bathing trunks and went out to sit on his steps that first afternoon and Myra Sears immediately came over and sat beside him. The prosecution had decided not to call her since the presence of Hutton at Steve's house had been admitted by the defense.

"Myra," said Steve, "think your father and mother could get along without you?"

Myra gazed up at him meltingly. "Oh, Steve," she said. "I couldn't get married yet. I'm too young."

"Of all the conceited little rabbits! I've been thinking about you in jail and I'm going to propose to your folks to let me send you to a boarding school."

"Oh," gasped Myra. "But it would cost a lot of money. You haven't any."

He grinned, "Any time I want it, I can get all the money I want."

"Would you come and see me some time?" she demanded.

"Sure. And you'd be home summers."

"Can I kiss you, Steve?"

"Behind the ears where you see the beauty spot."

"I won't." She threw her arms around his neck, kissed him on the mouth and then ran away shivering with shyness and happiness.

Steve rose and went in search of the General who was sitting in a chair in front of his cottage.

"Did they treat you good in jail?" the old man demanded.

Steve nodded. "I like it better out," he stated.

"You going to settle down, eh? The wind and the waves and the good earth."

"Nothing like them," agreed Steve.

"Course a young fellow ought to have a woman," remarked the Ancient. "They're a pasky nuisance but they got their uses."

"I don't feel the need at all."

"Hump. Lucinda Warburton's coming back tomorrow. She wrote me a letter. Her and me are good friends."

"Glad of it. Think I'll go for a swim."

"Don't like to talk about Lucinda," said Burton with a cackle.

"Bah!" retorted Steve.

THE FOLLOWING AFTERNOON about two-thirty, the vast bulk of Steve Cobb was stretched out on the pebbles just beyond the barrier of the Warburton place where all was soft sand. Steve was half dozing and half watchful but his eyes were closed when a slim graceful young person climbed over the barrier and stood over him.

A small bare foot touched his ribs. He opened his eyes.

"Oh, hello," he said casually.

Lucinda sat down beside him. Steve observed that the girl in the bathing suit was a trifle thinner and a bit pale but more beautiful than ever but he didn't say anything.

"I suppose you thought I treated you pretty rotten," she said slowly.

"Not at all. You were having a bad time."

"There was so many things you did that I couldn't understand," she said. "And father said you were all right, but wouldn't explain and I couldn't insist because he was so—so—sick."

"You loved your father, didn't you?"

She nodded and stifled a sob.

"Felt I was in a way responsible. If I hadn't broken through the wall of the barroom, Clews mightn't have fired."

"Why did you do that? Why were you hiding there? Why did you tie up Diana in the attic?"

"Lucinda," he said. "Let sleeping dogs lay. There was an antagonism between your father and me. It was ironed out. There was something he wanted me to do which I didn't want to do. We got together finally."

"I wanted so to write you. I wanted to come and see you. But I couldn't."

"How much did you pay Harvey Bellow for assisting my counsel?" he demanded.

"I—I—don't know what you're talking about. Of course I told Mr. Pennypacker to make sure you were protected. He said there wasn't a chance of your not being acquitted.

"But I suffered. I—I was outside the court the day of the trial."

"You precious child!" he exclaimed.

"I owe you so much. I never have thanked you about the kidnaping."

"Pshaw. It was nothing," he said much embarrassed. "Why did you come back to the Cape, Lucinda?"

"I wanted to. It's so lovely here. Restful, don't you think?"

"It was strenuous for a while, but it's fine now."

"I went on a cruise after father's death. The doctor said my nerves were bad. And on the cruise things sort of cleared up. All the weird things you did. Diana—"

"What became of her?"

"Nobody knows."

"So you finally decided you could stand seeing me?"

"Yes. I—I wanted to see you."

"Suppose you and I have a nice swim," he suggested hastily. "The water is fine."

"Steve, why did you rush after me and risk your life against those four wicked men?"

"You were a young girl in danger. Naturally a fellow had to do something about it."

"Oh," she said. After a second. "It wasn't because it was I, especially?"

"Why the very idea," he said, smiling.

"You haven't any money at all, have you, Steve?"

"It's like this, Lucinda. On the Cape you can live for almost nothing."

"If you loved a girl and she happened to be filthy rich, you'd never, never let her know that you loved her."

"Nope."

"If I were a man, I wouldn't let that stop me," she said sharply.

HE LOOKED AT her closely. "No, I can't imagine you as a man. You are unmistakably feminine."

"Do you know that we've never even had a friendly talk? You've been perfectly abominable on every occasion."

"When I think of some of the names you've called me, I positively squirm."

"Because you goaded me."

"Well we haven't abused each other today."

"That's because you're sorry for me. You don't need to be. I'm all over my grief and quite happy."

"Well, now, that's fine."

"I'd sort of like to be friends. To start fresh, as though you and I met for the first time and there weren't any painful things in the past."

"Nope," he said firmly. "I liked you when you were bawling me out. I love to remember the time when you set the servants on me and the other time when you went after me with a whip."

To his distress she began to weep. "And you paid me back by risking your life to save me from the kidnapers," she sobbed. "And I thought all the time you loved me."

He eyed her slyly.

"It made up for my affair with your stepmother?"

"You never had any affair with Diana. I know that," she exclaimed. "Steve, you're being as rotten as ever."

"Listen," he said sharply, "if you weren't so rich, and if you didn't mistake gratitude for affection, I'd—darned if I wouldn't kiss you."

Lucinda smiled at him bewitchingly.

"I'm in danger of losing all my money," she declared. "And I'm in love with a very rich man. I'm practically a pauper but if the man I loved kissed me and asked me to marry him, I would not hesitate a minute."

"Most women wouldn't. Men are different."

"A couple of days ago," said Lucinda pointedly, "Mr. Pennypacker came to see me. He said that you could talk all my money away from me if you wanted to—that you had some bonds or something that would ruin me if you demanded payment or something like that and that's why my father and you were fighting."

"Why the old fool," cried Steve indignantly.

"He said you were a fake beach comber. And he said you told my father to go ahead and do certain things and, now, you won't keep your share of the agreement. And, if you wanted to be nasty, I'd be penniless."

"So that's why you came down here?"

"I came down here to tell you to take the Warburton money if it belonged to you. I'd get along somehow. I don't want anything that doesn't belong to me. So I'm the beach comber, Steve. Aren't I?"

"Listen, Lucinda, how the deuce could you fall in love with a guy when you've only met him a few times and quarreled with him then?"

"How could you fight four men for a girl you hated?" she retorted.

He grinned. "Well the fact is I didn't hate you."

"So, now," said Lucinda shyly, "you've got all the money and what are you going to do about me?"

He leaned toward her. "This beach combing business is okay for a man, but not so nice for a girl. How about marrying me for my money, baby?"

"What are you marrying me for?"

"Well, frankly," said Steve with a most exasperating smile, "I want to kick Pennypacker, the old gossip, into the cold world so I'm willing to marry you just for that."

"Oh," cried Lucinda. She swung her right hand and slapped him smartly on the left cheek. Steve pushed her down on the beach and kissed her long and lingeringly.

Finally he sat up for breath. Lucinda sat up breathing heavily.

"Isn't there ever going to be any sentiment in our union?" she demanded, beaming brightly.

Steve pulled her over on his knees and squeezed her tightly.

"Just the same," she declared, "I won't ever marry you—until you say I love you."

"Oh, well," said Steve, "I love you, so what?"

"So I'll marry you almost any time," said Lucinda gleefully. "Kiss me again, lunkhead."

www.ingramcontent.com/pod-product-compliance
Lightning Source LLC
Chambersburg PA
CBHW030539030726
47495CB00004B/1059